He turned to leave and Katie blurted, "Luke, wait."

He turned, his dark brows lifting.

"I just wanted to thank you for coming to get me today. It meant a lot to me to be there. Honestly, I don't know how I would've gotten through it all if you weren't with me."

Then she reached up on tiptoes and pressed her lips to his cheek to give him a chaste peck, but suddenly her mouth moved and his mouth moved and their lips were locked in a real kiss. Luke made a sound from deep in his chest and a warm, delicious sensation sparked inside her.

She might've kissed Luke dozens of times in Vegas, but she didn't remember any one of them. This kiss she'd remember. This kiss she didn't want to end.

A moan rose from her throat, one of need and want.

Luke moved forward, backing her into the apartment, kissing her endlessly.

* * *

Vegas Vows, Texas Nights by Charlene Sands is part of the Boone Brothers of Texas series.

Dear Reader,

Welcome back to Boone Springs and the Boone brothers! How each one of these guys gets into female trouble is beyond me (ha!) but, this time, it's Lucas Boone who is finding it hard to keep his eyes and his hands off Katie Rodgers. Katie runs the Boone Springs bakery, Katie's Kupcakes. She's sweet, kind and compassionate, *except with him*. But he can't really blame her, not after the mistake they made in Las Vegas. Now Katie, the actual real girl of his dreams, is as forbidden as that ripe shiny red apple in the Garden of Eden. Katie is the baby sister of his ex-fiancée, a woman he practically left at the altar five years ago.

The only problem is that Luke can't get Katie out of his head. And he can't tell her the real reason he broke up with her sister. But they share a love of horses, which gives them common ground as they volunteer their spare time at the Red Barrel Horse Rescue.

Forbidden love always complicates things. Thank goodness for that, or we wouldn't have this story!

I hope you enjoy reading Luke and Katie's romantic adventure. It's a fun one. And I dare you not to fall in love with Luke!

Happy reading!

Charlene Sands

PS: Be sure to visit me at charlenesands.com, on Facebook, Instagram or Twitter.

CHARLENE SANDS

VEGAS VOWS, TEXAS NIGHTS

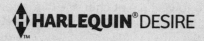

Recycling programs
for this product may
not exist in your area.

ISBN-13: 978-1-335-20884-2

Vegas Vows, Texas Nights

Copyright © 2020 by Charlene Swink

This edition published by arrangement with Harlequin Books S.A.

For questions and comments about the quality of this book, please contact us at CustomerService@Harlequin.com.

Printed in U.S.A.

www.Harlequin.com

Charlene Sands is a *USA TODAY* bestselling and award-winning author of more than forty romance novels. She writes sensual contemporary romances and stories of the Old West. When not writing, Charlene enjoys sunny Pacific beaches, great coffee, reading books from her favorite authors, and spending time with her "hero" husband and family. You can find her on Facebook, Twitter and Instagram. Sign up for her newsletter at www.charlenesands.com for ongoing giveaways, discounted books and new releases!

Facebook: www.Facebook.com/CharleneSandsBooks

Twitter: www.Twitter.com/CharleneSands

Books by Charlene Sands

Harlequin Desire

The Slades of Sunset Ranch

Sunset Surrender
Sunset Seduction
The Secret Heir of Sunset Ranch
Redeeming the CEO Cowboy

Boone Brothers of Texas

Texan for the Taking
Stranded and Seduced
Vegas Vows, Texas Nights

Visit her Author Profile page at Harlequin.com, or charlenesands.com, for more titles.

You can also find Charlene Sands on Facebook, along with other Harlequin Desire authors, at Facebook.com/harlequindesireauthors.

Dedicated to my lifelong friends: Mary, Allyson and Robin. Decades of Forever Friends, keepers of memories, hearts of gold, in good times and in bad, they are always there. We are fortunate to have each other.

One

Las Vegas, Nevada

Katie woke slowly, snuggling into her cushy pillow, her eyes refusing to open. A warming ray coming through the hotel room window caressed her skin, telling her it was later than her usual 4:00 a.m. wake-up-and-bake time.

But she wasn't in Boone Springs today and Katie's Kupcakes and Bakery was closed this weekend. She'd planned a super fun bachelorette party for her best friend, Drea, and fittingly, she'd just had the best dream of her life. Though the details were fuzzy, she'd never woken up with such delicious contentment before. From head to toe, her entire body tingled.

A nudge to her shoulder popped her eyes open. *What the...?*

"Sorry," a deep male voice whispered from behind her.

Her eyes opened wider as she tried to make sense of it. She hadn't imagined or dreamed the voice, had she? No, she was fully awake now, and it had been real. She could feel the warmth of the sheets beside her. A hand brushed over her bare shoulder and she gasped.

Oh no. She recognized that voice.

Taking the sheets covering her bare body, she rolled over, hoping her mind had played a nasty trick on her. But that hope was dashed the second she laid eyes on *him*, Lucas Boone—her sister's ex-fiancé, the man who'd crushed Shelly's heart.

Her stomach began to ache.

She clutched the sheets to her chin and sat up. That's when her head started pounding. "Luke, what on earth?" Dizzy, she swayed and struggled to focus.

"Sweetheart, lay back down. You drank me under the table last night and my head's aching like a sonofabitch. Your hangover's got to be much worse than mine."

"My...hangover? Luke, damn it. Is that all you have to say? Look at us! We're in bed together. And unless I miss my guess, you're as stark naked under the sheets as I am."

He reached for the sheet.

"Don't you dare look," she warned.

He set the sheet back down. "I guess you'd be right."

Her cheeks burned. Being in bed with Lucas Boone

was wrong on so many levels, she could hardly believe it. "What on earth did we do last night?"

Luke glanced at their shed clothes littering the hotel room and arched a brow.

"We couldn't have. I wouldn't… I couldn't…"

Goodness. She thought back to how Luke had called off the wedding to Katie's sister three days before the ceremony and had immediately enlisted in the Marines.

He'd claimed he wasn't ready to settle down and took all the blame upon himself, but that didn't make up for all the time he'd spent leading Shelly to believe they'd had a future together. That had been five years ago. Now Luke was living in Boone Springs again, the town founded a century ago by his ancestors. He was his brother Mason's best man, while Katie was maid of honor for Mason's fiancée, Drea. Unwittingly she and Luke had been thrown together in a joint bachelor/bachelorette party in Sin City. Vegas, baby. What happened here stayed here.

She thought about her sister again. How her scars remained. Poor Shelly faced the humiliation bravely but she'd never forgotten what Luke had done to her, how he'd betrayed her love and trust. She'd become bitter and sad and never let her mother, Diana, or Katie hear the end of how Luke had ruined her life. So the thought of Katie sleeping with Luke, her one-time friend, drunk or not, would be the worst of the worst.

Luke rolled over onto his side and braced his head in his hand, as if they were discussing what to have for breakfast. "What do you remember about last night?"

"What do I remember?"

"Yeah, do you remember leaving the party with me?"

She moved away from him as far as the bed would allow and thought about it. She remembered drinking and laughing and dancing with Luke most of the night. She'd felt guilty having so much fun with him, but they'd always gotten along, had always been friends until he'd backed out of the wedding.

The Boones had been good customers at her bakery. She and Luke also shared a love of horses and both volunteered at the Red Barrel Horse Rescue. Still, ever since his return from military service nearly a year ago, they'd been overly cautious with each other, their conversations often stilted and awkward. Katie, too, had been hurt when Luke had dumped her sister. Katie had also trusted him.

"I remember you offering to walk me back to my hotel." Which was only a few blocks away from the nightclub.

"We'd both had too much to drink."

The pain in her head was a reminder of that. "Yes."

Luke stared into her eyes; his were clear and deep blue. Kinda mesmerizing. "You pleaded with me not to take you back to your hotel. You didn't want the night to end. You…uh…"

Katie rubbed her aching head. This was getting worse by the second. "What?"

Luke remained silent.

"What did I say?" she demanded. She had to know, to make some sense out of this.

"You said you wanted what your friends had. You wanted someone to love."

"Oh God." She covered her face with her hands, her long hair spilling down. She was embarrassed that in her drunken state, she'd revealed her innermost secret desire. And to Luke no less. "And so we ended up in your hotel room?"

Luke flinched and his eyes squeezed shut. The concerned expression on his face really worried her. "Not exactly. We went somewhere else first."

"Another club?"

He shook his head. "Not according to this." He grabbed a piece of paper from his nightstand and gave it a once-over. "Another thing you said you wanted…" He handed her the paper.

She looked down at the bold lettering on the piece of parchment she held and her hand began shaking. A marriage certificate. Both of their names were listed and it had today's date. "You can't be serious."

"Hey, I don't remember much from last night either. My head's spinning like a damn top right now."

This was ridiculous. It had to be a bad joke. Where was the hidden camera? Someone was pranking her

Yes, it was true she'd thought of her secret wishes, often. She'd wanted to find love and be married, though she'd never voiced those wishes to anyone. She didn't want her friends to worry about her or think she envied their happiness, but she wouldn't have told Luke that, would she? Certainly she wouldn't have acted upon it.

Yet, the proof was staring her in the face. Dated today, as in they'd gotten married after midnight, about the time they'd walked out of the club together. The facts added up, but she still had trouble digesting all of it.

"I can't believe this. No, this isn't happening." She lowered her voice. "We didn't...do anything else, did we?"

Was she being naive to think that she'd end up naked in bed with handsome, appealing Luke without having sex with him?

"I remember some things. From last night." The blue in his eyes grew darker, more intense. "Don't you?"

She didn't want to. She didn't want to think it possible to spend the night with the one man in the whole world who was off-limits to her. But darn it, vague memories started to breach the surface of her mind. Being held, being kissed, her body caressed, loved. She grimaced. Dear Lord, the memories were fuzzy, vague, but they were there.

"Oh no," she whispered. Tears touched her eyes. "Why didn't you stop it?" she asked.

It was unfair of her to throw this all on him. The way he flinched at her question said he thought so, too. "I...couldn't."

He couldn't? What did that mean?

"Katie, it's going to be okay. We're married. I didn't take advantage of you. I mean, from what I remember, you weren't complaining about any of it."

She gripped the sheets closer to her chest. "That's what you think I'm worried about? It's okay that we had sex because we're married? My God, Luke. Do you have any idea how bad this is? You were engaged to my sister! You practically left her at the altar. My mom and sister were devastated. I'm not worried about my virtue here. It's way bigger than that."

"Okay, okay. Calm down." Luke ran a hand down his face. "I'm going to take a shower and get dressed and we'll discuss it. Unless you want to go first?"

"No, no." Married or not, she wasn't about to let him see her naked. "You go first."

"Fine. And Katie...it really is going to be all right."

She frowned. The frown only deepened when Luke rose from the bed as if they'd been married for years and walked into the bathroom, giving her a stunning view of his broad shoulders, muscular arms and perfect butt.

Her heart pounded hard. She'd married a Boone, one of the richest men in all of Texas, the man who'd betrayed her sister, the man she'd tried hard to avoid since he'd come back and resumed his life in Boone Springs months ago.

As soon as she heard the bathroom door close, she rose and scrambled to gather up her clothes from the floor. That's when she spotted an open condom packet, the top torn off, the contents empty. Now there was actual proof they'd consummated the marriage, as if her own sated body wasn't already screaming that to her.

She dressed and waited for him. They had to resolve this immediately. She wasn't going home as Katie Boone. No, sir. When she heard the shower faucet turn off, she braced herself, finger combing her hair, straightening out her cocktail dress, her resolve as sharp as her annoyance.

The door opened and out walked Luke, his hair wet, his skin glowing in the morning light. He wore a soft white towel around his waist, but the rest of him was hard, ripped muscle and brawn.

Good Lord. Was he the man in her dreams?

No, he couldn't be. Just because they'd once been friends and they shared a love of horses didn't mean she'd ever think of him that way, even subconsciously.

"Luke, we need to talk."

He looked her up and down, his eyes raking over her black dress, and suddenly she felt amazingly warm. She shifted her attention to a drop of water making its way down his bare chest, tunneling through tiny hairs to drip past his navel and absorb into the towel.

Luke caught her eyeing him and smiled. "I need a cup of coffee. We both do. I'll order breakfast while you take your shower."

He seemed too accommodating, too casual, as if he also hadn't made the biggest blunder of his life. Where was his panic?

"And we'll resolve this then?"

He nodded. "We'll talk, I promise."

Thirty minutes later, Katie stepped out of the bathroom refreshed and feeling a little better about her predicament. Her stomach still churned, but her outlook wasn't nearly as bleak. They were in Las Vegas, after all. How hard would it be to dissolve their quickie marriage, to seek a divorce from a wedding that should never have happened? Surely there were hundreds of people who found themselves in the same situation after a wild night and too much drinking.

Luke waited for her at the rolling table that had been

delivered by room service. Thankfully he was fully dressed now, in jeans and a navy shirt that made his eyes pop an even darker shade of blue. She had only the clothes she'd come with last night and her purse. Luckily her cell phone had enough charge for her to text Drea this morning telling her not to worry, she'd explain everything later.

Or not.

But she'd have to tell the bride-to-be something. They shared a hotel room and Drea had seen her leave with Luke last night and knew she hadn't returned to her room.

"Ready for breakfast?" Luke was already sipping coffee, the pot of steaming brew sitting on the table beside dishes of bacon, eggs, French toast, roasted potatoes and a basket of fresh pastries.

Ugh. None of it looked appetizing. She couldn't eat. "No, thanks. Coffee's good."

She grabbed the coffeepot and poured herself a cup, taking a seat facing him. She dumped in three sugar cubes and stirred, Luke giving her an arch of his brow. What could she say? She loved sweet comfort food and right now, sugar was her healing balm. His silent disapproval had her reaching for a fourth sugar cube, and she stared right at him as she dumped it into her coffee.

"You're not eating anything?" he asked.

"I'm not hungry, Luke. My head's still fuzzy."

"I thought the shower would help."

"The shower made me realize that if being in Vegas got us into this mess, then why can't being in Vegas get us out of it?"

Luke gave her a long stare and slowly shook his head. "What?"

"I want a divorce. Immediately. Surely there's someone in this city that can accommodate us."

Luke scratched his head, looking at her as if she were a child asking for the moon. "That's not possible, Katie."

"How can you say that? We haven't even tried. Look, I wasn't myself last night and you know it. How long have we known each other? Ten years?"

"Twelve and a half." She stared at him and he shrugged. "I have a good memory for dates. We met at the first anniversary of the Red Barrel Rescue."

Katie remembered that day. She'd chosen the rescue to be the subject of her high school term paper and had gone there not knowing what to expect. She'd taken one look at the beleaguered and maimed horses being cared for and had fallen in love. Luke had been a mentor of sorts, and through her, he'd met her sister, Shelly.

"And in all those twelve and a half years, have you ever known me to be impetuous or wild or, as you put it today, the kind of girl who could drink you under the table?"

"No." He scratched his head. "But then, I've never been with you in Vegas."

She rolled her eyes. "This is serious, Luke. I don't recall all that happened last night, but I do know we have to undo the problem as soon as possible."

"I...agree."

"You do? Good, because for a second there, I was starting to believe you didn't think this was a big problem."

"I can't get a divorce until I speak with my attorney. I'm sorry, Katie, but this isn't going to happen today."

"Why not?"

"Because it's more complicated than that. I'm a Boone, and that means divorce proceedings can get pretty nasty. My attorney isn't going to let me sign my name to anything until he sees it."

"Goodness, Luke, I don't want anything from you or your family. If that's what you're getting at, you can go straight to—"

"It's not me, Katie. It's just the way things are when you're…"

"Rich?"

"A Boone."

"How horrible it must be for you not knowing who you can trust. I suppose you had those very same issues with Shelly?"

"Let's leave your sister out of this."

"Easy for you to say." Katie's stomach burned now, the acid churning violently. This was not going well. He was being obtuse and the implication that she was somehow out for Boone money only ticked her off. "There's nothing we can do? Maybe if you give your attorney a call—"

Luke frowned. "I can't. He's out of the country on a personal matter."

"Personal matter? You could say this is your personal matter."

He sighed. "His mother is extremely ill and he's there to help get her affairs in order. That is, if the worst happens."

"Oh. I'm sorry to hear that. Can't you use someone else?"

Luke shook his head. "I'm afraid it doesn't work that way. At least not for me."

She jammed her hands on her hips and his attention immediately was drawn there. Gosh, how much of last night did he remember? He was looking at her differently than he ever had before. As if he was taking their marriage seriously, as if she was…his wife. "I can't go back to Boone Springs married to you, Luke."

"Looks like you're going to have to. Our flight leaves in a few hours."

Katie sighed and tears welled in her eyes. "I can't believe this."

He kept silent.

She had no choice but to relent. She saw no other way out. If she prolonged her stay here in Las Vegas, the entire wedding party would get suspicious. She didn't need that. She had to keep what happened between her and Luke quiet. She'd think of something before the Boone company plane took off.

"Fine. I'm not happy about this. If the truth comes out, I'm doomed. It'll ruin my relationship with my family. And who knows how this would affect my mama's health. Promise me that no one will know about this, promise me you'll keep our secret."

Luke touched her hand, his slight caress sweet, comforting and confusing as hell. "I promise, Katie. No one will know."

Luke waited until everyone boarded the Boone company plane, keeping his eyes trained on Katie. She took a seat by the bridesmaids in the back, all the girls huddling around the bride-to-be.

He couldn't keep from admiring Katie's beautiful blond hair tied up in a ponytail, the strands framing her face making her look wholesome and sweet. She was all those things, but last night at the club, he'd seen her flirty, passionate side. Mischief had glowed in her soft green eyes, especially while she'd been dancing in her sexy black dress. Now, in a denim jacket and jeans, she contrasted beautifully with the creamy leather seats and ambience of the custom designed plane.

She was his wife now. He could hardly believe it. He was actually married to Katie Rodgers. While Mason was engaged to Drea and his other brother, Risk, was engaged to April, Luke had inadvertently beaten his brothers down the aisle.

Katie glanced his way and their eyes met. He could look at her forever and never tire of it. But as soon as she caught him eyeing her, she turned away.

He smiled inside but didn't dare appear content around a quiet, sullen Katie. She was just cordial enough to her friends to ward off questions. She'd told everyone she'd gotten sick last night, barfing up her brains and Luke had taken her to urgent care in the wee hours of the morning to make sure she wasn't dehydrated. It was a feasible fib, one everyone seemed to believe, with the exception of his brothers. While Drea had thanked him for taking care of her best friend, both Risk and Mason had given him the stink eye.

Hell, he certainly hadn't planned any of this, but hearing Katie's softly spoken desire about wanting love in her life, wanting to be married, had reached down deep inside him and wrung out his lonely heart. He'd been drunk, too, and his willpower around her had been at an all-time low. She'd flirted with him, practically asked him to make love to her, and well…he didn't have much defense against that. Not with her.

The pilot, a navy veteran, came by to say hello to the passengers and make sure everyone was ready for takeoff.

Luke shook his hand. "Hey, Bill. Hope you didn't lose too much at the tables while you were here."

"Nah, my big gambling days are behind me. The penny slots are just my speed."

"I hear you," Luke said. He'd never been a gambler. He didn't like to play games he couldn't control. And he didn't like the odds in Las Vegas, with the exception of his recent marriage.

The odds of him marrying Katie had been slim to none. Yet he'd beat them and no one was more surprised than he was. Except Katie. He'd won the jackpot and now he had to convince his new bride being married to him wasn't a big fat mistake.

"Any time you want to come up and copilot, you know where the cockpit is," Bill said.

"Maybe later. Right now I'm still feeling the effects of last night's party." Luke grinned. "I'm afraid you're the designated driver today." He was in no shape to navigate anything, much less fly the friendly skies. He'd become a helicopter pilot while living on Rising Springs Ranch and had gotten his pilot's license in flight school during his stint in the service. Yet Mason had insisted he not pilot the plane so Luke could let loose and not have to worry about his alcohol consumption. His brother wanted everyone to have a good time.

"Sure thing. I'll see that you all have a good flight."

"Thanks, Bill."

Luke buckled up and glanced back at Katie. She was all set, looking like she'd just lost her best friend, even though Drea was sitting right next to her.

He sighed and as he turned his head around, he came eye to eye with Risk in the seat beside him. "Something going on between you two?" he asked.

He'd promised Katie he wouldn't give away their secret and he wouldn't betray that vow. "Who?"

"Don't be obtuse. You and Katie."

"No, nothing."

"I'm not judging," Risk said. "And if you do have something going with her, it'd be a good thing. I can read you like a book. You're hot for her."

Luke shot him a warning look.

Risk's hands went up. "I'm just saying, if you get together with her, you have my approval."

"Like I'd need it."

"Hey, just want to see you happy for once."

"You do know who she is, right?"

Risk smirked. "The best pastry chef in all of Texas. She'd keep us silly in gourmet cupcakes."

"She's Shelly's younger sister. And she barely tolerates me."

Years ago, Katie had dragged Shelly to a Red Barrel charity function and had introduced them. There'd been instant attraction between them and Luke had begun dating Katie's big sister. The engagement had seemed to fall right into place. Until the day Luke had woken up and realized he was making a big mistake.

"You two took off together last night," Risk said, "and today, you can't take your eyes off her."

"Leave it alone. Okay?"

Risk seemed to read the emotion on his face. "Okay, I'll back off." He slapped Luke on the shoulder. "But if you run into a problem, I'm here for you."

"Appreciate that. Why aren't you hanging with your fiancée?"

"Seems the girls won't call it quits on their bachelorette party until the plane touches down in Boone Springs."

Risk eyed April, giving Luke a chance to seek out Katie again. And there she was, trying her best not to spoil everyone's fun, trying to smile and conceal the pain she must be going through. The thought that he was the cause of her pain ate away at him. It was the last thing he wanted. But he couldn't let her go. Not now.

She was the girl who shared a love of horses with him, the girl he'd danced with most of the night, the impossible girl who'd been in his dreams for the past five years.

He needed a chance with her, and this was the best he was going to get.

One chance.

Was that too much to ask?

Two

A Boone limo picked up the entire wedding party at the airport, taking everyone directly to their homes on the outskirts of town. Katie was among the last to be dropped off since she lived in the heart of Boone Springs, her apartment just above the bakery. It was a modest place, with one bedroom, one bath, but the rooms were spacious enough and her large home kitchen served as a backup when orders in the bakery exceeded their limit. That didn't happen often. Katie ran an efficient place and there was nothing like rolling out of bed at 4:00 a.m. and working in her jammies downstairs until the bakery opened at seven o'clock.

As the limo pulled up in front of the bakery, she was struck with a pang of relief. "This is my stop," she said to her friends remaining in the limo. "I hope you all had a great time."

Drea gave her a big hug. "It was wonderful. Amazing girl-bonding, my friend. Thanks for all you've done. Love you for it."

"Love you, too."

Katie glanced at everyone and waved a farewell. "All of you made the party for our dear friends something to remember."

"After last night, I've forgotten more than I remember," Mason said, smiling.

"You had the best time with your friends and family, especially with your fiancée." Drea gave him a quick kiss on the cheek. "Just ask me, I'll fill in the blanks."

Katie had some blanks she'd like to have filled in, too.

"One thing I do know, Luke and Katie worked hard on organizing this. Thank you," Mason said. "You two make a good team."

A rush of heat crawled up her neck. "Thank you. It wasn't that hard, really, and it was fun." The only difficult part had been working with Luke. *Her husband.* Oh God.

The limo driver grabbed Katie's bags and opened the door for her.

"I'll get off here, too," Luke told the driver.

Katie glared at him.

"It's a short walk to the office," he explained. "And I need to check up on something. Benny, if you could drop off my bags at the ranch I'd appreciate it."

The limo driver nodded. "Yes, sir."

Katie climbed out, Luke right behind her.

"I'll take those." He grabbed her bags from the driver's hand.

Katie noticed some raised eyebrows in the limo and wanted to melt right into the cement. What on earth was Luke doing? She didn't want to arouse suspicion. It was bad enough she'd had to lie to her best friend about where she'd been last night. But Luke was oblivious as to how his behavior appeared to everyone.

"Bye," Drea said. "Thanks again, hon. We'll talk soon."

"Okay," Katie said, giving her friend a smile.

When the limo drove off, she turned to Luke. "Give me my bags, Luke."

"I'll carry them up for you."

"That's not necessary."

"I know, but I'd like to."

"Why?"

"Your hangover is hanging on. You're pale and looking a little weak."

"The only reason I look ill is because of what happened between us. Makes me sick to my stomach."

His mouth twitched, but she wasn't at all sorry she'd been so crude. Well, maybe she was a little bit sorry. This was just as much her fault as it was his.

"All the more reason for me to help you. I feel responsible."

"Don't."

"I can't help it, Katie. C'mon, you need to rest."

She didn't like him telling her what she needed, but

his jaw was set stubbornly and they couldn't stand here all day arguing. "Okay, fine."

He had the good sense not to gloat at winning the point. He nodded and walked over to the front door with her bags.

She opened up her shop and walked in first. The bakery had been closed for three days, yet the scent of vanilla, cinnamon and sugar flavored the air. The smell of home. She sighed and her body relaxed.

"Smells like you in here," Luke remarked, as if reading her thoughts.

"How's that?" she asked.

"Sweet."

She let his comment hang in the air for a moment. She didn't feel sweet right now. She felt horrible and guilty. She kept wishing she could escape from this horrible dream. Waking up wed to her sister's ex was truly a nightmare. And the sooner they rectified it, the better.

"The stairs are in the back, through the kitchen." She led the way and he followed.

He stopped to take a look at her baking area. "So this is where the cupcake magic happens. I've always wondered what this place looked like."

"Yep, this is it. This is where I spend a good deal of my life." She couldn't keep the pleasure out of her voice. She was proud of her shop, proud of what she'd accomplished. And she loved her work.

Luke took in the huge mixer, bowls and cupcake tins, the bins of flour and sugar and the industrial-size refrigerator. Yes, this was home to her.

"I see you here," Luke said, as if he was picturing her at work.

"It's not glamourous."

"I would imagine it's darn hard work. But work that you enjoy."

"True."

"Your bakery is the best in the county, everyone knows that. But I've only known you as a horse lover. You spend a lot of time at Red Barrel. How do you find time for both?"

"You run a multimillion-dollar company, how do you find the time?"

He grinned. "You're quick, I'll give you that."

"Apparently, not quick enough," she mumbled. Or else she wouldn't have gone to bed with him.

Luke ran a hand down his face. "I wasn't lying when I said it was mutual, Katie. I know that for a fact. Don't blame yourself too much."

She squeezed her eyes shut briefly and nodded. The man she knew at the horse rescue was gentle and caring and kind. He'd been her friend at one time and that was where it all got confusing. Because he had hurt her sister and maybe what Katie thought she'd known about him was all wrong. "Okay, can we just not talk about it?"

"Talk about what?" He played along. "You were going to tell me how you find time to work at the rescue."

"My workday ends early. And I think the work we do at the rescue is important. Those animals need help." She lifted a shoulder. "I don't date. Or at least I haven't for a while and so I have all kinds of—"

"You won't be dating, Katie."

She didn't like his tone, or the implied command. "Luke, for heaven's sake. You think I want to complicate my life even more?" She fisted her hands. "And you don't get to tell me what I can or cannot do."

"It may have been a hasty wedding, but you're my wife."

She wrinkled her nose. "Don't say that."

"I'm your husband."

"For a nanosecond. Remember, you promised that you'll look into a divorce as soon as possible."

"I said it and I will. But until that time..." Luke came closer, his incredible eyes soft on her. He took her hand and squeezed. "If you ever need anything, call me."

"You know what I want."

He smiled and his blue eyes darkened. "I know what you think you want."

"What does that mean?"

His hand gently wrapped around her neck, his fingertips urging her forward. Then he lowered his mouth to hers and kissed her. It was tender and sweet, not at all demanding, and the pleasure made it hard to pull away.

"I think you should leave," she murmured, pushing at his chest.

"I was just going."

When he backed away, she stared at him. There was a moment, one tiny second, when she saw something in him that made her happy, made her wish he didn't have to go.

"When you hear from your attorney, give me a call."

He nodded and walked out of the bakery.

Maybe it was a good thing she hadn't taken him up to her apartment.

"Here's your herbal tea, Mama." Katie handed her mother a mug and took a seat beside her on the living room sofa in the home Katie and her sister had grown up in on Blue Jay Avenue. The neighborhood was close-knit, just on the outskirts of Boone Springs, about a ten-minute drive from the bakery. She'd come here as soon as she'd unpacked her bags.

"Thanks, honey. I love the pomegranate and black-berry mix." Her mother blew on the steam and then sipped delicately. "Mmm. Tastes so good going down."

"It is good," she said, concerned over her mother's health.

Diana Rodgers had tired eyes that told of sacrifice and lack of energy. Her body was a bit broken from ill health. At the age of fifty-eight, she'd suffered a minor heart attack that had taken her away from the teaching job she'd loved. Taking an early retirement had never been in her plans. She'd been a single mother most of her life, working hard at the grammar school with special needs kids. But the job was stressful, and Diana often took her work home with her, a habit her cardiologist couldn't condone.

"So why aren't you joining me in a cup?"

"I will a little later. Right now, I just want to hear how you're feeling."

"You've only been gone three days, hon. I appreciate you coming over as soon as you got home, but I'm the same as I was before you left." Her mom waved her hand. "Enough about me, how was your trip?"

"It was…nice." Katie had trouble mustering up any enthusiasm. *Oh, and one little detail I forgot to mention… I married Lucas Boone.* "Drea and Mason enjoyed it very much. I think everyone did."

Her mother moved around in her seat a bit and her mouth twisted as it did every time the Boone name was mentioned. "Too bad Drea had to fall in love with *him*."

"Mom, Mason's a nice guy."

"He's rich and feels entitled, just like all the Boones." She meant Luke.

That sick feeling in Katie's stomach acted up again. "Drea's happy and that's all that matters."

Her mother sipped her tea. "So, what did all you gals do at the bachelorette party?"

Katie shrugged. "The usual things. We saw the sights, ate like there was no tomorrow, had a spa day, went to a concert, and then on the last night the entire group got together for a party at a nightclub."

There. She'd given a short, encapsulated version of her long weekend. Enough said.

"You had to deal with Luke?"

Before she could answer, Shelly walked into the house, dropping her shoulder bag on the edge of the sofa. "What about loser Luke?"

Katie's heart started pounding. Shelly was still bitter. "Hi, sis. What are you doing here?"

"Checking in with Mom, just like you." Her sister, dressed in nurse's white, walked over to give her mother a kiss on the cheek. "Hi, Mom. How are you today?"

"Feeling pretty good. Your sister made me some tea. Would you like a cup, sweetheart?"

"Thanks, but I'm fine. Just thought I'd stop by here first, before heading home and changing clothes. Dr. Moore asked me and a few colleagues to attend his seminar tonight. I have to leave soon. So, what about Luke?"

"Nothing," Katie said.

"Your sister had to plan Drea's bachelorette party with him."

"We didn't plan the bachelorette party together. He was in charge of entertaining the groomsmen. All we did was coordinate the party at the end of the weekend together."

"Ugh," Shelly said. "Poor you."

"It wasn't that bad."

"I feel sorry for any woman who gets involved with him," Shelly said flatly. "I should've known better."

"He wasn't ready for marriage," Katie said. God, they'd had this conversation for years. It was truly beginning to grate on her nerves. Shelly never was one for letting go. She'd never forgiven their dad for divorcing their mother. She'd never accepted their father's new wife. Clearly, a broken engagement, even if it was three days before the ceremony, was much better than a divorce later on.

"Why are you defending him?" Shelly asked.

"Maybe I just want you to move on with your life, Shel. Maybe I'm not defending him so much as I'm looking out for you."

Shelly sighed. "Okay, got it. Easier said than done."

"It's so nice to have both of my girls here with me today," her mother said softly.

"I wish I could stay longer," Shelly said. "But I'm meeting everyone at the hospital in an hour."

"That's fine, honey. You go on to the seminar. I'm proud of the way you girls are so conscientious about your work. That means you, too, Katie."

"I know, Mama." Her mother had always told her how proud she was of what she'd accomplished at the bakery. Her business was on solid ground now but it hadn't always been that way. Her mom had faith in her, had always given her support. "I'll stay and visit with you a bit longer."

"Wonderful." Shelly gave her a rare smile.

Her sister had had a rough time facing her friends after the marriage debacle and then to have her "almost" groom leave town for years, leaving her with no hope, no way to reconcile her sadness, no way to rant and rave at him. That was probably the greatest injustice. Shelly had never gotten the closure she'd needed.

After Shelly left, Diana got up to take her teacup to the kitchen. "I made soup, your favorite, chicken and dumplings. Will you stay and have some with me?"

"Sure, that sounds yummy."

Katie was beat, tired and nervous, but having comfort food and her mother's company would distract her from the giant mistake she'd made in Las Vegas last night.

Katie raced down the stairs, stubbing her toe on the last step. "Ow, damn it." As she entered the bakery, not even the soothing scents of all things sweet helped lighten her mood this morning. She'd overslept by an hour and now she was totally behind schedule. Gosh, she'd had so much on her mind, sleep had eluded her, and when she'd finally fallen asleep, it had been deep and heavy. She'd dreamed that a faceless beast was chasing her and she'd kept running and running until she'd woken up in a sweat.

Was that dream trying to tell her something?

She flipped on the light, tied on her lavender Katie's Kupcakes and Bakery apron and got to work, gathering up her ingredients, prepping her cupcake tins.

The Monday morning special was always a carrot zucchini cupcake infused with a light apricot filling. She called it her Start Smart Special, a healthier alternative to a sugary treat. It was a fan favorite for those guilty of indulging over the weekend.

Her assistant, Lori, knocked on the back door. Katie opened it to her smiling face.

"Hey, good to see you. How was your trip?" Lori asked, as she walked past her and took off her sweater.

"Uh, it was okay."

"That so? Just okay?" Lori sounded as if she had her doubts. They'd worked closely together for six years and knew each other pretty well. Now Lori was putting herself through college at night aiming for a degree in business, so the bakery hours were perfect for her. The shop closed at two in the afternoon. "Sounds like it wasn't fun. Did something happen?"

"No. Nothing. I'm just tired. I overslept."

"You never oversleep. Maybe you had *too* much

fun in Vegas." Lori winked. If she only knew. "You're gonna have to give me deets. I've been cramming all weekend, stuck at my place, fantasizing about your fun weekend."

"There are no details." Katie shrugged. "We had a good time. Saw a show. Got massages, did some dancing. Usual stuff."

"You were excited about it when you left here. I thought for sure you'd have some good Vegas stories to entertain me with this morning."

Lori put on her apron and they began measuring out ingredients. She started on chocolate ganache cupcakes with marshmallow filling while Katie worked on the special. They had their routine down to a science and being behind schedule meant one or two cupcakes would have to get the boot.

"Sorry, Lori. Nothing much to report," she fibbed. "How about we eliminate anything pumpkin, since the fall season has been over for a while," she said, changing the subject.

"Good choice."

"And if there are any complaints, you know what to do."

"Always."

It was her motto to keep the customer happy by giving away a free cupcake or two to ward off hostility. Although that rarely happened with her regular Boone Springs customers. They were like family. She knew most of them by name, as well as where they lived and how many kids they had. She often catered birthday parties and other occasions.

While the cupcakes were baking, she worked on pastries, filling croissants, making cookies and cinnamon rolls. Between the two of them, working nonstop, they'd filled the bakery case shelves by 7:00 a.m. Coffee brewed and her regulars began popping into the shop.

By nine thirty, there was a lull and Katie flopped into a chair in the small lounge by the back door. Exhaustion set in and it wasn't just from lack of sleep, but acute mental fatigue over what happened in Vegas this past weekend.

Lori gave her a sympathetic look. "Why don't you go upstairs for an hour?" she suggested. "Get in a nap. I can handle things until it picks up again."

"Don't we have deliveries today?" Sometimes they'd get orders from companies or restaurants or clients celebrating big birthdays.

Lori scanned the list on the bakery wall. "It's Monday and pretty calm right now."

"Thanks, but I'll be fine in a few minutes. Just need to get a second wind."

The second wind didn't come and by closing time, Katie was truly beat. She had one delivery to make, a last-minute order for a private dinner party happening later tonight. They needed a dozen tiramisu and a dozen lemon raspberry cupcakes, and while Lori closed up shop, Katie arranged the cupcakes in a box and taped it shut.

"Let me take those for you," Lori said. "I can drop them off on my way home. This way you can go upstairs now and relax, put your feet up."

"I can't let you do that. You've got studying to do."

"It'll take me ten minutes, tops. It's my way of making up for all the days you let me off early when I had to cram for an exam. Say yes."

"You really are such a good friend. Yes. Thanks."

Lori smiled. "Welcome."

After Lori took off with the delivery, Katie climbed the stairs slowly and once inside her apartment, plopped down on her sofa. She turned on the television, struggling to keep her eyes open until she finally lost the battle.

Normally, Luke spent most of his time in the office in the main house at Rising Springs Ranch. He took a hands-on approach to running things on the property and had a good relationship with Joe Buckley, their ranch foreman. They worked well together and Luke knew Joe wouldn't let him down.

Today he was at the Boone Springs corporate office, sitting in a room with his name plaque on the desk, staring out the window.

He had Katie on the brain and he'd come into town today, just because he wanted to be close to her. Her bakery was only two blocks away, nestled in between a clothing boutique and a fabric store. Because of the location, the bakery got pretty good foot traffic. Even if it didn't, Katie would be successful, because her pastries were the best in the county and because Luke had made sure no Boone holdings would ever compete with her.

A little fact he'd kept secret.

While he was serving the country, he'd made his wishes known and his brothers had all been onboard.

He'd put the Rodgers family through enough and they'd done what they could to make sure Shelly and her family wouldn't unintentionally suffer any hardships of their doing.

But for him, it had mostly been about Katie. Wanting to see her succeed, wanting her to have a good life. God, when he'd come back home, he'd wished she had married, or at the very least, been in a serious relationship. Knowing she was still single had made his return torturous, yet he'd managed to keep his distance when he saw her around town or when they volunteered at the horse rescue.

And then Vegas happened.

Frustrated, he forced himself to go over ranching reports he'd pulled up on his computer. He had to get some work done, had to feel productive today, instead of daydreaming about seeing Katie again.

A little after two in the afternoon, his cell phone rang. "Hey, Wes. How's it going?" Luke usually didn't hear from the manager of the horse rescue, so he knew this had to be important.

"Hey, Luke. Sorry for the call, but it's Snow. I'm sorry to say it might be her time. The ole girl isn't breathing real well. I've had Dr. Hernandez out. He gave her some painkillers, but that's about all he can do for her. Thought you'd like to know."

Luke's stomach churned. Snowball was a mustang who'd been severely abused and she'd come to the rescue at the same time he'd returned home. He and Katie both had sort of taken the mare under their wing. They had a soft spot for the old girl. She'd been recovering, but the abuse had taken its toll on her and unfortunately with some of the horses, there wasn't much else to do but ease their pain.

"Thanks, Wes. Sorry to hear that. I'll, uh, I'll come by. I want to see her."

"Thought you would."

"I'll let Katie know, too."

"I just called Katie. She didn't answer her phone. I left her a message."

"Okay, well, I'll try to get word to her somehow. I'll see you soon, Wes."

Luke hung up and rubbed at the corners of his eyes. Giving himself a moment to gather his thoughts, he shook his head. As much as he wanted to see Katie again, he didn't want to give her bad news.

Five minutes later, he was in his car, driving by the bakery. There was a Katie's Kupcakes Is Klosed sign on the window. Still, he parked the car in a diagonal spot right in front of the bakery and got out. He tried the shop's door handle. No luck. Then he cupped his hands to ward off the sun's glare and peered inside the window. Not a soul was around.

A car slowed on the street and a young girl called out, "Can I help you?"

He recognized her as one of Katie's employees, though he couldn't recall her name. She'd made a few deliveries to the Boone corporate office. "I'm looking for Katie."

"Hold on a sec." The young woman parked her car and walked over to where he stood by the door.

"I'm Lucas Boone."

She smiled as if to say she knew who he was; the Boones were usually recognized in town. "Hi, Lucas. I'm Lori. Do you need cupcakes or something? The bakery is closed."

"No, nothing like that. I need to see Katie. It's important. Has to do with the Red Barrel Horse Rescue."

"Oh… I see." The young woman nibbled on her lips.

"She's not answering her phone."

"No, she's probably resting up in her apartment. She was pretty exhausted today."

"It's really important. Can you help me?"

She thought it over for a few seconds. "I know your brother is marrying her best friend, Drea. So, I guess it's all right if I let you in."

"Thank you."

Lori put the key into the lock and opened the door. "I only came back because I left my textbook and notes here and I've got this big exam tomorrow night."

Luke nodded and she let him inside the empty bakery.

"I'll go upstairs and knock on her door," she said. "I'll let Katie know you're here."

And a few minutes later, Luke was face-to-face with a sleep-hazy Katie.

"W-what are you doing here?" Katie stood at her doorway, a plaid blanket wrapped around her shoulders, staring at Luke. She didn't think she'd see him again so soon. His head was down, a concerned look on his face. Her heart began to pound hard. "Lori said something about the rescue?"

"I got a call from Wes a little while ago. It's Snow. She's in bad shape."

The air left her lungs and her shoulders slumped. "Oh no. Not our girl."

"Yep. I'm afraid so." He rubbed the back of his neck. "Thought you'd want to know. Wes tried to call you."

"I—I was fast asleep. I didn't hear my phone."

"I'm on my way out to see her. Maybe for the last time."

Oh man. All she could think about was the raw deal Snowball had gotten, a life of abuse and pain. Her owner had neglected her and she'd come to the rescue undernourished, scarred and broken. It wasn't fair. They'd tried their best to save her, and now Katie wasn't about to let her take her last breaths alone. "I've got to see her, too."

"I'll take you."

"No, you go on." She ran a hand through her hair. She must look a mess. "I need to run a comb through my hair and freshen up."

"I'll wait."

"You don't have to."

"Katie, I'm here, my car's out front and we're driving to the same place. Let's not waste any more time when we can spend it with Snow. Just do what you have to do, I'll be waiting downstairs."

He was right. Snow was too important to her to quibble with him about driving arrangements. "Okay, fine. Give me a minute."

Five minutes later, she was dressed in jeans and a red shirt, her hair in a knot at the top of her head. She splashed water on her face and put on lip gloss to keep from biting her lips and then dashed down the stairs and out the door of the bakery.

Luke waited for her out front, leaning against his black SUV, his hands in his pockets, a pensive look on his face. Her stomach was still in a twist about her ultra-secret marriage to her sister's ex. And now, the sweet mare she'd tended for the past year might be dying.

"Ready?" Luke asked, opening the door for her.

"Yes... I think."

"Yeah, I know what you mean. Snow's a special one."

Katie climbed in and grabbed her seat belt while Luke closed the door and took a seat behind the wheel. They drove off in silence and as they approached the canyon, she shivered.

"Cold?" he asked.

"A little." She hugged her arms to her chest. "I forgot my jacket." She'd forgotten how chilly the canyon could get in the later hours of the day.

"I can warm you up real fast," he said, giving her a smile.

His dimpled grin brought heat to her body instantly. She flashed back to Vegas and those hours they'd spent in bed together.

He reached for the dials on his dashboard and soon a flow of warm air surrounded her. "Better?"

She nodded.

"I've got an extra jacket in the back. I won't let you freeze to death out here."

That he was talking about "letting" her do anything or not gave her nerves a rattle. He wasn't really her husband—just thinking it seemed completely foreign to her—but he was taking care of her needs and that wasn't something she was used to, with any guy. "Thanks."

A few minutes later they approached Red Barrel Horse Rescue and Luke parked in the gravel lot in front of the small building that served as the office. "I'll go in and let Wes know we're here," he said. "You want to stay in the car and keep warm?"

"No, I'll go with you."

"Sure," he said. He stretched way back and grabbed two jackets from the back seat of his car. "Here you go."

He handed her a suede jacket lined with lamb's wool, while he took a lighter weight cotton one. They tossed them on, hers almost reaching her knees, and Wes came out of the office to greet them.

The men shook hands, then Wes gave her a gentle hug. "I knew you two would come out as soon as you heard. Snow's in the barn. I've made her as comfortable as possible."

Luke met her eyes, then looked back at Wes. "We'd like to see her now."

"You two know the way. Stay as long as you want."

"Thanks," Luke said, his hand closing over hers gently. They began walking toward the barn and Katie took note of all the other horses in the corrals on the property. They were the lucky ones who'd been given a second chance at Red Barrel. There were so many others who were sick and hungry running wild in the canyons.

Once they reached the wide wooden doors, Luke

turned to her. "No matter what happens in there, just know we did the very best we could for her."

"I know that," she whispered. "It's just that she's a special one. And she's been through so much."

"Well then," he said, his eyes softening. "Let's make her final hours the best they can be."

She held on to a breath. And then exhaled. "Okay."

They walked out of the daylight and into the darkened barn. A cold shiver ran through her. It was definitely jacket weather in the canyon.

"There she is," he said, pointing to the largest paddock in the barn.

Katie moved closer to the stall and as she laid eyes on Snow, she clutched her chest. "Oh, sweet girl." It hurt so much seeing Snow weak, giving up the fight.

"She's down," Luke said. "But she's still with us."

"Yes, she still is. You've waited for us, haven't you, my pretty Snowball?"

Snow lifted her head and eyed them both before laying her head back down on a pillow of straw.

Katie took off her jacket and entered the stall, laying the jacket on the straw beside the mare. "Do you mind?" she asked Luke.

"Not at all," he said, doing the same with his jacket.

They lowered down and sat on the jackets next to Snow.

"Hey, girl. I'm here," she whispered in her ear. "You don't have to do this alone." Katie laid her hand on Snow's mane and used the gentlest touch to comfort her. "I know you're struggling to breathe. Just stay calm. I'm here."

Luke stroked Snow's flank and whistled a soft, mellow

tune. He was actually pretty good and not only did the whistling relax the mare, it soothed Katie's nerves as well.

"That's nice," she said, closing her eyes. "How did you learn to do that?"

"A buddy of mine taught me when I was overseas."

Katie opened her eyes. "When you were in Afghanistan?"

He nodded. "We had time to kill when we weren't on active duty. You know, something to fill the void from being away from home."

"Must've been hard."

"It wasn't a walk in the park," he said.

"Yet you signed up for it. When you had family here and a multimillion-dollar company to run. You didn't have to enlist."

"I felt like I did. I think the time away helped."

"Are you talking about my sister now?"

He nodded. "I never meant to hurt her. I know she hates me, but a lot of time has passed since we broke up."

"You mean, since you walked out on her? Humiliated her?"

"Yeah," he said, frowning. "If that's the way you want to put it."

"It's just that my family trusted you," she said, stroking Snow's mane. Luke hadn't stopped his caresses either. "And your decision sort of came out of left field."

"What can I say that I haven't already?"

Katie was at odds with her feelings. She wanted to support Shelly and their mom, but Luke had a point. He couldn't marry a woman he didn't love. It was just too bad he'd come to that conclusion right before the wedding was to take place.

"I know they hate me, Katie. But do you?"

The question took her completely off guard. "*Hate*'s a strong word."

"So you don't?"

"Let's just say I hate how things played out."

Luke nodded. "Fair enough."

"Speaking about the way things played out, any news from your attorney about our dilemma?"

Luke frowned. "No."

She drew a deep breath. "Too much to hope, I guess."

Snow became agitated, moving around on her bed of straw.

"I think you need to keep whistling," Katie said. "It really does help her."

Luke put his lips together again and the melodic sounds filled the barn. Soon, Snow calmed and her breaths came more evenly.

Afternoon gave way to evening, and the ole girl hung on. Snow's eyes were closed now, her breathing more labored. "That's my girl, Snow. Ease over the bridge now. You'll be in a better place soon." Katie bent to kiss her and stroked up and down her nose.

Luke took a break from whistling. "I remember when I first spotted her. She was covered with sores and bruises, yet she had soulful eyes. They were filled with such life, such hope."

"I was appalled at the way she'd been treated. For heaven's sake, the poor thing didn't have a name," Katie said.

"Yeah, I remember. Her coat was black underneath the dirt, and that circle of white on her forehead right smack between her ears couldn't be missed. It looked like she'd been struck by a fat snowball."

"And I named her Snowball."

"I named her Snowball," Luke said, raising his voice an octave.

She smiled, seeing the feigned indignation on his face. In truth, she didn't know who'd said it first, but they'd agreed on the name. "Okay, maybe we both named her Snowball."

Luke smiled, too. "I think that's the way it happened. Finally, we agree on something."

Katie liked this Luke, the one who showed compassion. A man who could laugh at himself and not put on airs. He was a zillionaire, yet he never seemed to flaunt it. "It's the magic of Snow. She's…"

They both gazed down at the mare. She was still. No longer breathing. "Oh no."

Katie looked at Luke as both their smiles faded. The mare had taken her last breath as they were conversing. Snow had heard them, recognized their voices and felt at peace enough to slip away without struggle.

Tears stung Katie's eyes.

Luke, too, was pinching the inner corners of his eyes. "She's g-gone."

"She is," he said. He wrapped his arms around her shoulders, pulling her in close. "But she went knowing she was loved."

Katie couldn't hold back any longer. She nodded, bobbing her head as the truth of his words sank in.

She wept quietly and turned to Luke, her tears running down her cheeks and soaking his shirt.

"It's okay, Katie. Don't cry, sweetheart."

"I knew this day would come, but I didn't think it would be so soon. I thought we'd have more time with her."

She had never owned a pet. She'd never had an animal to care for, to nurture and love, until she'd started working at the rescue. She loved all the horses here; they all had a story. But for some reason Snow was special. She'd touched Katie's heart and they'd shared a deep connection, a bond that she didn't have with any of the others. Katie had taken it as a personal challenge to make Snow's days comfortable.

Luke clearly felt the same way. His eyes moist, his expression sad, he couldn't mask his sorrow either. He brushed his lips across her forehead. She needed his warmth right now, his strength.

"There's nothing more we can do." His voice was shaky and he seemed reluctant to release her, to let go of the bond they'd shared. "We should go."

She nodded, wiping her face with the back of her hand and then attempting to pat his shirt dry from her tears. "Sorry."

"Don't worry about it," he said softly.

"I hate to leave her."

"I'll let Wes know she's gone. He'll take good care of her from now on."

It was hard to let go. To say goodbye.

Luke rose and helped her up, entwining their hands. "Ready?"

"I think so." She glanced at poor Snow one last time, her heart breaking.

Luke picked up the jackets and brushed the straw off them. "Put this on. It'll be cold outside."

He gave the fallen horse one last glance, too, a look filled with sadness and regret as he grabbed a woolen blanket from the stall post and covered her body.

Katie slipped into his jacket and he clasped her hand again, his warmth and strength seeping into her. He led her out of the barn. "C'mon, sweetheart. Let me take you home."

She didn't mind the endearment this time; she couldn't fight it. Couldn't argue. She'd had a rough twenty-four hours and she was just too numb to think anymore. His shoulders were there for her to lean on, he seemed to know the right things to say and this one time she would accept what Luke had to offer.

Without guilt.

Three

Luke stood facing Katie at the threshold of her apartment. He'd insisted on escorting her upstairs after entering the bakery, probably because she couldn't quite get her emotions in check. She'd wept most of the drive home, little sobs that broke from her lips every time she pictured Snow lying still on the ground, lifeless. In the car, Luke had glanced at her often. She'd felt his concerned gaze but she couldn't look him in the eye. She didn't like showing her vulnerable side to anyone, but tonight she couldn't help it. Her emotions were running out of control.

"Are you going to be okay?" he asked her.

"I think so." She bit her lip. "You don't have to worry about me."

He stared into her eyes, then ran a hand down his jawline. "But I do."

"You have no obligation to me, Luke. Really, I'll be fine."

"Is that what you think this is?"

He said it softly, without condemnation, and suddenly she felt small and petty. "No, no. I'm sorry. I know you're just as upset as I am about Snow. Really, I'm glad we shared her last night together. You cared for her as much as I did. Gosh, I can't believe I'm speaking of her in the past tense."

"It's strange, huh?"

"Yeah."

She stared at him, so many thoughts racing through her mind. But mostly, she was glad he was there tonight, lending her comfort, helping her come to grips with losing Snow.

"It's been a long day. I should let you go, get some rest," he said.

"That sounds…good."

"Okay, well. Good night then."

He turned to leave and Katie blurted, "Luke, wait."

He turned, his dark brows lifting.

She took both of his hands in hers and gave a squeeze. "I just wanted to thank you for coming to get me today. It meant a lot to me to be there. Honestly, I don't know how I would've gotten through it all, if you weren't with me."

Then she reached up on tiptoes and pressed her lips to his cheek to give him a chaste peck, but suddenly she turned her head, he turned his, and their lips were locked in a real kiss. Luke made a sound from deep in his chest and a warm delicious sensation sparked inside her.

She might've kissed Luke dozens of times in Vegas, but she didn't remember any one of them. *This* kiss she'd remember. This kiss she didn't want to end.

A moan rose from her throat, one of need and want, and for a moment she flushed, totally embarrassed. But Luke didn't stop, he didn't hesitate to devour her mouth. He was all in, too, stirring her deepest yearnings to be held, to be comforted. She was hurting inside and this kiss was a balm to her soul.

He moved forward, backing her into the apartment, kissing her endlessly. She went willingly, relishing the taste of him, the raw pleasure he was giving to her. He tossed his jacket off and then removed hers without breaking the kiss. Then he cradled her in his arms, holding her so close to him that his need pressed against her belly.

A surge of heat raced through her. It was astonishing how quickly he made her come alive. She was glad of it, glad of the sensations rocking her body. In Luke's strong arms, she suddenly wanted what was forbidden to her.

"Luke," she said when the kiss came to an end.

He looked deep into her eyes. "Don't tell me to stop," he whispered, grazing his lips over hers again.

"I'm not, but maybe we should come up for air?"

The quick smile on his face devastated her. He was so darn handsome. Why did it have to be him? She took a deep breath, pausing for just a few seconds. "Okay, that's enough."

"You're good with this?" he asked, brushing a wayward strand of hair off her face. "Don't answer that," he murmured. "I already know you are."

He cupped her face in his hands and gazed into her eyes, before claiming her lips again. The absolute pleasure overwhelmed her, helping to ease the pain in her heart. It amazed her how easily she welcomed him, how much she wanted more of his kisses, more of him. Her insides heated, and a spiral of warmth traveled through her body, making her hot, needy.

"You feel it, too, don't you?" he whispered in her ear.

She shouldn't. But yes, yes. She did. "Yes," she said softly, hating to admit it, but she couldn't lie to him. Couldn't try to deny how his touch shockingly turned her on. How his kisses made her melt. How she wanted more.

This was all about Snow and the loss she felt. It had to be. Because no other reason would do.

Luke unbuttoned his shirt and tossed it off. He clasped her hand and set it flat on his chest. The taut muscles under her palm intrigued her and she moved her hand over him, gently mapping out the broad expanse of his chest. He was stunning, hard, firm, tough.

Electricity sizzled between them, an invisible connection pulling her closer, making her head swim. She pressed a kiss to his shoulder and felt him shudder.

"Katie."

Her name came from deep in his throat, not a plea, not a warning, but a mixture of awe and reverence that set off a barrage of tingles.

She hadn't had a man in her life for two years, and even that hadn't been anything serious, just casual dating. And now here she was with Lucas Boone, for heaven's sake, wanting him, needing his strength and compassion. Her body reacted to his, and she was sure it was mutual grief heightening the sensations, making a hard day a bit easier.

He began kissing her again, drawing her tight into his arms, his big hands caressing her shoulders, her back and then lower yet. Everything below her waist throbbed in the very best way.

She moaned, a guttural sound erupting from her throat that she didn't recognize as her own. Yet she relished the way Luke touched her, and soon his hands were caressing her chest, undoing the buttons on her blouse, pushing it off her. His eyes gleamed as he took in her small round breasts overflowing the cups of her bra.

"So beautiful," he murmured between kisses.

His praise brought more tingles, more heat. She was lost in the moment, totally and fully engaged. He removed her bra and cupped her breasts, taking one into his mouth, stroking it with his tongue gently, reverently, making her feel more alive than she'd ever felt before.

Soon she was wrapped in his arms and being carried into her bedroom. He didn't let up, didn't stop kissing her until he set her down, her boots touching the ground.

"Invite me in," he rasped.

That made her smile. "You're already here," she whispered.

His lips quirked up in a sexy way and she wouldn't have been able to deny him, even if she'd wanted to. "I guess I am." He kissed her again and before she knew it, the rest of her clothes were off and she lay waiting for Luke on the bed.

She had a moment of panic, the realization of what was happening finally dawning. This was Luke, her sister's ex, the man she'd accidentally married in Las Vegas. Yet she'd bonded with him tonight while they were saying goodbye to Snow and shared a deep loss together. It was complicated, and she'd deal with it later, but now...now she needed the comfort he provided. The thrills were an added bonus.

He came over her on the bed, gazing down, a hungry look in his eyes. "I don't take this lightly, Katie. I... This isn't—"

"I know," she said simply. "I know why this is happening."

"You do?"

"It's about Snow."

Luke stared at her for a long second. "Yeah."

Then he covered her body with his, stroking her below the waist until she whimpered in pleasure and then shattered into a hundred pieces. Now she knew what total bliss felt like and she basked in contentment. "Oh wow," was all she could say.

"Yeah, wow," Luke said, pressing tiny kisses along her shoulder blades, allowing her time to enjoy the aftermath of her climax.

Then he brought his lips to hers again, and she welcomed it and invited him in with her body. He wasted no time shedding the rest of his clothes and sheathing himself in a condom. "I want you, Katie."

She knew. And so when he joined their bodies and gasped, she did, too. "Oh, Luke."

He filled her full and the need inside her grew as his thrusts deepened. Each movement heightened the intensity until she cried out. Luke seemed as lost as she was, moving inside her in a deliberate rhythm that lifted her hips and took her completely home.

He wasn't far behind. His thrusts grew harder, his face masked in pained pleasure and she kept pace with him, taking the ride with him, until he finally shuddered in release.

Moments later, he fell upon the bed next to her and cradled her in his arms. He kissed her forehead and kept her close, both of them too out of breath to utter a word.

Luke woke first, and Katie's sweet scent wafted to his nose. He felt her presence beside him on the bed, and when he opened his eyes and actually saw her snuggled in tight, her honey blond strands spilling onto her pillow, he smiled. She was his wife, and they'd made love last night like they belonged together. This was his honeymoon, all he'd ever wanted. All he'd ever needed.

How many lonely nights had he spent thinking about her? During his stint in the Marines, forbidden thoughts of her would creep into his mind. He'd felt terrible for hurting Shelly, for hurting the Rodgers family. But it would've been a whole lot worse, being married to one sister while secretly craving the other. Often, when he was alone with his thoughts in Afghanistan, he'd wondered if he'd been a damn fool for falling for a woman he'd never touched, never kissed. How would he know if they were compatible? What if the real thing didn't live up to the fantasy?

Now, he knew.

Oh boy, were they compatible. Katie *was* his real thing, his fantasy come true.

He stared at her, watching her take slow peaceful breaths. He should probably leave and let her come to grips with what happened alone. But he couldn't walk out on her. He couldn't leave without seeing her reaction. Was he a fool to hope that she'd be okay with what happened between them?

It was nearing 4:00 a.m. She'd soon be rising for work, but he needed a few more minutes to savor being in bed with her, to savor the sweet serenity of her body next to his, their warmth mingling.

Luke sighed and bent over to place a light kiss on her cheek.

"Mmm," she murmured in her sleep.

He smiled and gently moved a fallen strand of hair from her face. "My pretty Katie," he whispered, needing to touch her again.

She tossed around a bit and he backed off, turning to his side and bracing his head in his hand, content to just watch her sleep.

Too soon, the alarm clock on the nightstand blasted through the peace and Katie opened her eyes and found him beside her. "Hi," she said.

Her greeting surprised him.

"Morning, sweetheart."

Clearly, she wasn't thinking straight.

Luke reached over her to shut off the alarm and then

pressed his luck, brushing his lips over hers. Her lips were warm and welcoming. For a second, he held on to hope. "Did you sleep well?"

She blinked and blinked again. "What the…" And then she darted up on the bed, a pained expression on her face. "Oh no."

She glanced down, obviously noting she'd slept in the nude. She grimaced as if her world was coming to an end and then covered up her perfect body.

"Katie—"

"Luke, this was only about Snow. We were both hurting last night, but I… I should've known better. I shouldn't have let my emotions overwhelm my judgment. We can't keep doing this."

"Seems to me, we *do* keep doing this. Must mean something."

"It does. It means I'm a numbskull."

"No, you're not. You're human, and you have real feelings that you can't chuck away or hide. It was good between us last night."

Katie stared at him as if remembering. She couldn't deny the sparks and fire they'd shared last night. For him, there was nothing better.

"Yes, but it can't happen again. We were both…lost."

He wasn't lost. He'd known exactly what he'd needed. And she did, too, but she wouldn't admit it.

She shrugged and a little pout curled her mouth up. "Poor Snow."

"Yeah. It was hard losing her, but you gave her the comfort she needed."

"You really think so?"

He nodded. "I think you're amazing."

"Don't say things like that. It's already complicated enough."

"What, I can't praise my wife?"

She gritted her teeth. "I…am…not…your…wife."

Luke's good nature faded. Why was the thought of being married to him so distasteful? Of course, he knew it was because of Shelly, but was that all it was? Her harsh tone spurred his temper. "Funny, but I have a document that says you are. And, sweetheart, we've consummated our marriage more than once already."

"Don't remind me," she said, rising from the bed, taking the sheets with her. But one corner of the sheet caught on the nightstand knob and jerked away from her body. She stood before him naked in all her glory.

She hoisted her chin. "I'm taking a shower. I'm already late getting to the bakery. You need to leave before Lori gets here, which is in less than an hour."

As she turned away, he focused on the curvy shape of her bare body, her rounded cheeks and the length of her long legs.

It was a freaking turn-on. His throat went dry and his body grew immediately hard. Hell, he wasn't getting out of this bed until he calmed down. He needed to think about cattle prices or something equally benign.

And ticked off as he was, he still couldn't help wondering what she would do if he followed her into the shower.

Katie set two pots of coffee brewing on the back counter of the bakery, behind the near empty bakery case. Normally, decaf was her speed, but this morning she needed a large jolt of caffeine, something that would make her think more clearly. Obviously, last night she'd had no clarity. Not one bit. All she'd had was grief and Luke's welcoming arms.

Spending the night with him had been a big mistake, but at the time she'd needed someone. No, not just someone... She'd needed Luke.

God, she didn't want to feel things for him that would cause a world of trouble. What she'd confessed to him in Las Vegas was true. She wanted someone in her life. She wanted a partner, someone to share moments with, someone who'd have her back. But it couldn't be him. Never him. Her mother's weak heart couldn't take it and Shelly would probably disown her as a sister. She held Luke responsible for her lack of trust in men and her generally bitter disposition.

Katie felt sorry for Shelly and was completely guilt-ridden about finding momentary pleasure in Luke's arms last night. He was the poison apple and she'd taken the forbidden bite.

Katie set out her utensils and staples: bowls, measuring cups, flour, sugar and eggs. She had begun measuring out her ingredients when the sound of boot heels clicking on the stairs reached her ears. Her nerves rattled a bit. It was Luke. Thank God, he was leaving.

"Coffee smells real good. Mind if I have a cup?" he asked.

She kept her head down, pouring sugar into the industrial-size bowl. "It's not ready yet."

"That's okay. I'll wait."

She glanced at the wall clock.

"Don't worry, I'll be out of your hair in a few minutes. I just want a little coffee before I head out. Lori will never know I was here."

"But I will," she muttered.

Luke chuckled.

"Don't laugh. None of this is funny."

He came up behind her, his nearness making her jittery. "Katie, I'm not laughing at the situation. I know this isn't easy on you. I'm laughing, because…well."

"What?" She turned to face him. He'd cleaned up nicely, his dark blond hair groomed and overnight beard extremely swoon-worthy.

He curled his hands around her waist and drew her in with those sky blue eyes. "You're cute when you're angry. Sexy, too."

"Hardly, Luke." She rolled her eyes.

"You doubt it, after last night?"

"Look, I know you think you're my husband and all, but from now on, I'd appreciate it if you didn't tell me I was amazing or sexy or cute. I'm none of those things…to you."

"Sounds like the coffee's ready." He ignored her comment and walked into the bakery.

She sighed. Maybe it was better not to argue with him. He would leave soon and she could go on with her baking.

"You want leaded?" he asked from the other room.

"God, yes," she called to him.

While he was pouring coffee, she combined all the ingredients for her base cupcake recipe and turned on the mixer. Then she started cutting up fruit for her fresh fillings; it was peaches and apples today.

Luke walked in with two steaming cups of coffee. "You take anything in it?"

"No, just black is fine," she said. She sampled too many of her sweets during the day to add any more sugar to her diet. She'd learned the hard way to always taste test her pastries before putting them on the shelves.

"I like watching you work," he said, handing her a cup.

She didn't know what to do with that comment. She clutched the cup to warm up her hands and wished he'd just leave.

"Do you get up at four every morning?"

She nodded. "If I want to open the bakery at seven, I do."

"It's a lot of work."

"It is, but Lori's a big help. Most mornings we're right on schedule."

He smiled, then sipped his coffee. He made her uncomfortable, eyeballing her the way that he was. She put her coffee down and got back to work.

"Okay," he said, taking a huge gulp. "It's time for me to get going, too."

"So soon?" she asked with a rise in her voice and once again, he chuckled.

"You know, I can stick around if it'd make you feel better."

"Out," she said, turning her back on him.

Luke didn't seem to take offense. Instead he roped

his arms around her and she turned to frown at him. "What are you doing?"

"Giving you a goodbye kiss."

And then his mouth was on hers, and the melding of their lips felt like heaven on earth.

When the kiss ended, she backed away from him and pointed to the door. "Go."

He went.

She drew a deep breath and then let out a flustered sigh. Whenever the man kissed her, she felt helpless and needy.

It was all so terribly wrong.

Three days later, Drea entered the bakery just before lunch, a big smile on her face. Her bestie was smiling a lot lately and most of that had to do with Mason. Katie wasn't jealous of their happiness; she was thrilled for the two of them. It was just, at times, she thought she'd never meet the right guy, never know that kind of love.

She didn't get any encouragement from her sister and mom. They both thought a woman was better off without a man, but Katie didn't see it that way. She wasn't bitter or jaded, not yet anyway. But being around that sort of pessimism made it hard to keep a positive attitude.

Drea walked up to the counter and Katie greeted her. "Hi there. What brings you by so early this morning?"

"I have an invitation for you."

"Lunch? I'd love to." She wouldn't mind catching up with her friend.

"No, silly. Not lunch. Mason and I want to thank

you for helping us plan the wedding and for being the best bachelorette party planner around. We want to take you to dinner tonight. Don't say no. We really, really want to do this."

Katie smiled. "Of course. I'd love to. Thanks."

"Can you be ready by six?"

"I can." She gave Drea a nod. Well, it wasn't lunch with her friend, but Mason was a pretty nice guy and Katie could use the distraction. "Where should I meet you?"

"Oh, no need for that. Luke will pick you up."

"Luke? Uh, why on earth?"

Drea shook her head. "Listen, I know he's not your favorite person, but you two seemed to get along just fine in Las Vegas."

The mention of Vegas brought up visions of their hasty drunken marriage and Katie's stomach squeezed tight.

"It's a thank-you dinner for him, too. We thought you wouldn't mind…much. I mean, you two have been working together at Red Barrel, right? And you seem cordial enough lately."

Oh gosh. Little did Drea know, Luke made her uncomfortable in too many ways to name. Being cordial to him in public was an act.

Yet Katie didn't want to come off as a scrooge. She didn't want to hurt Mason's feelings either, by refusing to break bread with his brother. What could she say? She was trapped, by no conscious doing by her friend. "No, that's fine. But maybe I should drive myself. You know, in case it's a late night. I wouldn't want to hold you guys up. You know I turn into a pumpkin by ten o'clock."

Drea laughed. "I promise Luke will have you home by ten."

"Can't we all go together?"

"We could, only Mason and I will be leaving earlier in the day for a final meeting with our wedding caterer and we didn't think you'd want to be dragged to that."

It was an impossible set of circumstances. Having maid of honor duties alongside Luke as best man, they were bound to be thrown together, but Katie hadn't seen this one coming. Not by a longshot. "Fine, have Luke pick me up. What should I wear?"

"Something dazzling. We're going to The Majestic."

It was a swanky non-Boone restaurant known for its classically romantic atmosphere on the outskirts of Boone County. "Nice," Katie said, feigning enthusiasm.

"Okay, great. We'll see you tonight." Drea clapped her hands. "I'm so excited. I've never been there before."

"Neither have I."

"It'll be a first for both of us then."

At noon, Katie and Lori were in the midst of their second rush hour, the first always coming around eight in the morning. This noon rush wasn't anything they couldn't handle, so when Shelly walked in with a man by her side, Katie greeted them both.

"Hi, Shel. Good to see you. What's up?" She darted a glance at the good-looking blond man standing beside Shelly.

"Katie, this is Dr. Moore. He's new in town and I told

him about the best cupcakes in all of Boone County. Dr. Moore, this is my talented sis, Katie."

They exchanged greetings.

"Let me warn you, I have a sweet tooth," Dr. Moore said. "So you might be seeing me in here a great deal."

"Then you are my kind of person. Welcome. Do you have a favorite flavor?"

"I told him you make the best lemon raspberry cupcake in the world." Shelly smiled and there was a light in her eyes that Katie hadn't seen in a long time.

"Sounds good to me. Love the shop, by the way," he said, admiring the pastel decor and dining area. He glanced at the bakery case. "And it looks like I'll be back to try everything you have in here."

"Good thing his brother is a dentist," Shelly said, teasing.

Katie chuckled. Her sister *never* teased, at least not recently, and it brought a lightness to Katie's heart. "I'd say so. So, will you two be eating here? We also have coffee, hot chocolate and chai."

"Another time. I'm afraid I have to get back to the hospital ASAP."

"Me, too," Shelly said.

"Okay then, let me box these up for you. And I'll throw in a few of my carrot zucchini specials and my newest creation, vanilla infused with peaches."

"That's very nice of you. Can't wait to try them later." His cell phone rang and he glanced at the screen. "Excuse me. I'm sorry, but I have to get this," he said, walking toward the front door. "Shelly, can you meet me outside?"

"Of course."

"Thanks again, Katie."

"Sure thing."

The second the doctor walked out, Katie couldn't hold her tongue. "He's really cute."

"I suppose."

"You mean to say you haven't noticed?"

Shelly caught her drift and rolled her eyes. "Oh, for heaven's sake. I was just being neighborly. Dr. Moore doesn't know too many people in town. I thought he'd like the shop and I wanted to introduce him to you."

"So, you're not interested in him? Because he seems nice and you've never brought a guy into my shop before this."

"No, I'm not interested in him. Luke ruined me for all men, I'm afraid. So don't even think it."

"Shel, really. It's been years and it's time you moved on. Can't I think it a *little bit*?"

"Not even a smidge."

Katie sighed. She only wanted her sister to be happy. But it looked like Shelly was fighting it tooth and nail.

Katie selected the cupcakes from the bakery case and set them in the box, sealing it with two Katie's Kupcakes stickers. "Okay then. Here you go," she said, handing the box to Shelly.

"Thanks for the treats, sis."

"Shel?"

"What?"

"I like it when you come by to see me. You should do it more often."

Shelly's expression softened and there was beauty in her eyes and her smile just then. "I will. I promise."

Katie watched her sister leave and sighed. She had her own problems to deal with.

Tonight, she had a "date" with the man who'd broken her sister's heart.

Four

Luke scrutinized his reflection in the mirror after changing his shirt and tie several times trying to get the look just right. Normally, he didn't give two figs about looking sharp, but tonight he was going on a date with Katie. Well, not a date, but hell, the way his stomach was doing somersaults, it might as well be one. He hadn't seen her in three days. He'd kept himself busy, but no amount of work or play could keep him from thinking about her.

Once dressed, he headed to the parlor and found Aunt Lottie sitting on the sofa, all alone, sipping from a tumbler of bourbon. As soon as she noticed him, she gave him a wolf whistle and he chuckled. He never knew what she would do or say. She was genuine and quite a surprise and that's why all of his family loved her. But the desolate look he'd caught on her face moments before he entered the room tugged at his heart.

"You look handsome, Luke. Got a hot date?"

"Thanks. And you know I'm going to dinner with Mason and Drea tonight."

"And Katie, too? Is that why you've spruced up?"

"Never mind me. What's wrong, Aunt Lottie? And don't put me off. You've been unusually quiet lately. Is it Drew?"

She pursed her lips, but then finally nodded. "That man's got me all mixed up."

Drew MacDonald lived on the property now. He'd once been a land baron, with a ranch adjacent to Rising Springs, but he'd fallen on hard times when his wife Maria passed away. Lottie and Maria had been dear friends, and now years later, Drew and Luke's aunt were testing the waters of a relationship that unfortunately seemed to be drying up.

"It's clear you two care for each other."

"I suppose," she said. "But he's forever badgering me about this and that."

"That's nothing new. Even when Maria was alive, you two didn't much see eye to eye."

"Isn't that important though? Seems to me, a man and woman should have the same disposition."

"Boring."

"What?" she asked.

"Aunt Lottie, I know you. We all do. You have an adventurous nature. If you two got along like steak and potatoes, there wouldn't be any sparks. He's spirited, and you certainly are. Makes for a pretty lively union, if you ask me."

"I don't know. I always feel like I'm too much for him. Like he wants me to change."

"Does he tell you that?"

"No. But it's quite apparent to me."

Luke shook his head. "I don't know about that. I think he cares an awful lot for you. And you have deep feelings for him, too."

His aunt blinked. "The last time we were together was at the Founder's Day gala. We fought and he walked out."

Luke knew about the argument. Drew had been upset at Lottie for putting her life in danger, running into the street trying to save a wayward dog. And April, Risk's fiancée, had pushed her out of the way before a car almost hit her. It had all been caught on video and had made the news.

"That was a couple of months back."

"I know. Now, whenever we see each other on the ranch, it's awkward and we barely speak."

Luke took his aunt's hand. "You're a wonderful woman and I'll always have your back, but I can see Drew's point of view, too. He doesn't want you taking unnecessary risks."

"I made it all these sixty-two years."

"But he lost a wife. He's probably very sensitive about this stuff."

Lottie nodded. "How'd you get so smart about these things?"

"I wouldn't say I'm smart. I have issues." The biggest one being he'd married a woman who wanted out, as quickly as possible. And he was dragging his feet. "But I had a lot of time to think when I was in the service. Four years' worth. I guess you could say I see the big picture now and something's telling me that you two should go for it."

"You really think so?"

He nodded. "Yes, I think so. You're both being stubborn."

"I'll keep that in mind. Thanks," she said, giving him a kiss on the cheek. "Now, go. Have a great time with your Katie."

His aunt gave him a coy look. Sometimes he wondered if she had uncanny powers of perception.

"I'm going. I'm going."

From the minute Katie stepped into The Majestic, she felt transported into another era. The black-and-white-checkered floors, the elaborate table dressings with fine bone china and tiered, flickering candles gave way to sophistication and romance from a time long ago.

"You fit in this place, Katie," Luke said. "Especially tonight. I like your hair up like that."

She didn't want to hear his compliments. When he'd picked her up at her bakery apartment, he'd given her compliment after compliment, making her head swim, giving her ego a boost. True, she'd gone all out, putting her hair up in a messy bun, dressing in a long sleek black gown with a slit up the side and a thin rope of delicate rhinestones stitched into a sloping neckline.

She'd bought the dress at an estate sale in Dallas. It was a gown she'd had to have, yet she'd never believed she'd have a place to wear it. Until tonight.

"This place is beautiful," she said, in awe of her surroundings.

Boone County appealed to many, but this place was one of a kind and definitely catered to the rich and fabulously famous.

"Like I said, you fit in perfectly."

She took his arm and stared into his deep blue eyes. Wearing a slate gray suit, his dark blond hair smoothed back showing off his strong jawline, he wasn't exactly hard on the eye. But that was shallow of her. He was much more than that. Mostly, he was off-limits. "Thank you. But please don't say nice things like that. This situation is hard enough."

She hoped her plea would set him straight. After hearing Shelly's bitter comment today about Luke ruining her for all men, Katie had to keep a firm resolve. There was too much at stake and she had to admit that Luke's compliments were charming her. Making her want things she had no right wanting.

"I'm only speaking the truth," he said in his defense.

"You see, that's what I mean." She squeezed her eyes closed for a moment. "Just don't. Please, Luke."

His eyes shuttered yet he didn't answer her.

The maître d' greeted them. "Mr. Boone, so good to see you again. Please, follow me. I believe your brother and his fiancée are waiting for you."

Luke pressed a hand to her back and guided her farther into the restaurant. It was only a moment before she spotted Drea and Mason sitting at a corner table overlooking the patio gardens. Thank goodness. She needed reinforcements tonight. Drea would make the perfect buffer.

The maître d' showed them to the table and pulled out a chair for her. She took her seat and Luke sat down next to her, his scent, his presence looming. She'd been intimate with him and was beginning to learn his mannerisms, like how his eyes turned a darker shade of blue when he was turned on, and how his mouth twitched when he tried to hide a smile, and how when he was exasperated, he'd run a hand along his jawline. She'd seen that one a lot since Las Vegas.

"Hi, you two." Drea smiled at them.

Mason reached over to shake Luke's hand. "Glad you both could make it."

"Thanks for the invite," Luke said.

"Yes…thank you," Katie added, though she'd rather muck a barn stall than spend any more time with Luke.

"Isn't this place spectacular?" Drea asked. "I feel like I'm in a 1940s movie or something."

"I feel the same way," Katie said.

"The food here is top-notch," Mason said. "The owner, Billy Meadows, was a friend of our father's. I think Henry Boone would've loved to top this place in grandeur, but Dad wasn't the greedy type. He saw his competition as a good thing."

"It's good for the town, too," Katie said. "Having choices, that is."

The Boone brothers gave each other a quick glance. Katie wondered what that was all about, but quickly

Luke changed the subject. "So, your wedding is in less than a month. Hard to believe. If there's anything I can do for you guys, let me know."

"Same here," Katie interjected.

"Don't you worry, Katie my friend," Drea said. "I have a list of things I need help with. My final gown fitting is coming up and the bridesmaids' dresses are in."

"Exciting. Sign me up," Katie said.

"Aren't you helping Aunt Lottie with the bridal shower?" Luke asked her.

"Yes. And I'm looking forward to that. It's next weekend." Drea wanted a couples shower, and that meant more contact with Luke, but oh well, there was nothing Katie could do about it. Once the wedding was over, and Katie and Luke were properly divorced, she wouldn't have to spend any time with him.

"I feel bad taking you away from Red Barrel," Drea said. "I know you like to spend your free time there and it seems like I'll be usurping all of it."

"I...don't mind." The reminder of the rescue disheartened Katie. She hadn't been back since Snow died. "It's part of my MOH duties."

"That's maid of honor, in case you two didn't catch on," Drea added.

Mason smiled at her. "We're not that slow. I knew what it meant."

"Good thing you did. Because I had no idea," Luke said.

"You're not up on wedding speak, bro." Then Mason turned to Katie. "You looked sad when Drea mentioned the rescue. So sorry. Luke told me you lost a precious mare not too long ago."

"Yes. It was hard. She was a special one."

Drea's voice softened. "I've already told you how sorry I am that you lost Snow."

Luke touched her hand and she gazed into his eyes, seeing the compassion there. "She's at peace now."

Katie nodded, then pasted on a big smile. She wasn't here to bring everyone down. Yet the reminder of losing Snow, combined with her sister's bitterness today, gave her a stomachache. "I'm fine, really. Drea, I've been your friend since third grade and I'm looking forward to every minute of helping you with your wedding plans, so don't you worry about putting me out. We've fantasized about this day for as long as I can remember."

Drea blew her an air-kiss. "I know we have. And your day will come, too, and when it does, I'll be right there for you."

Katie's cheeks heated and she felt like such a fraud, sitting here next to her best friend and lying through her teeth. She couldn't even spare Luke a glance for fear of giving herself away.

Luckily, the waiter approached with menus and took their drink orders.

"Nothing for me please. Just water." She couldn't take a drink, not with her stomach in turmoil. And she'd sort of sworn off alcohol ever since Las Vegas.

Once the drinks were served, Mason asked everyone to raise their glasses. "Thank you both for coming. We wanted to show our appreciation for giving us a wonderful party in Las Vegas. Everyone had a good time, thanks to you both. Drea and I really appreciate your love and support. So, here's to a loving family and lasting friendships."

Everyone clinked their glasses and sipped. Then Drea gave Luke a kiss on the cheek and turned to give Katie a big hug and kiss, too.

"It was my pleasure," Katie said.

"Yeah," Luke said. "My pleasure, too. It was a great time for everyone."

Katie didn't have the heart to agree with him. It would be the biggest lie of all.

Musicians set up beyond the dance floor and began playing tunes her grandparents had probably loved. It was lively, big band stuff that seemed to bring out the best in people. After the waiter came by to take their orders, Mason grabbed Drea's hand and pulled her onto the dance floor. Drea turned to give Katie a helpless look as if to say sorry for leaving her alone with Luke.

"Would you like to dance?" Luke asked, after a minute of silence.

She shook her head. "No, thanks." She didn't want Luke holding her, touching her. They'd done too much of that already. Her stomach still churned and the only thing that would make it better was to be free of Lucas Boone. When she was sure Mason and Drea were well beyond hearing distance, she whispered, "I need an update on…on our divorce."

"What?" Luke leaned closer to her and she repeated what she'd said into his ear. His pure male scent filled her nostrils, and her mind flashed to the night they'd shared together. She wished those memories would fade, but every time she was close to him, they became sharper.

"I don't have an update. My attorney is still out of the country."

"Shh." Why was he using his regular speaking voice? "Surely there's something we can do," she said quietly.

Luke took her hand. "Sorry, Katie."

She didn't want his apologies, she wanted action. She could try to find an attorney herself, but unless she ventured to Willow County or some other town, she feared news would get out. It was the curse of living in a small town: the gossip hotline was long. Luke had promised her his attorney would use great discretion and she believed that, because nobody wanted to cross a Boone.

She pulled out of his grasp, but not before Drea and Mason returned to the table and eyed their linked hands. *Oh boy.*

Mason's brows rose, but dear Drea pretended not to notice.

After dinner was served, the conversation around the table was pleasant and engaging. Mostly they talked about wedding plans and the building of Mason and Drea's new home on Rising Springs Ranch property.

"Katie's going to help me design our kitchen," Drea said. "She's the expert in that area."

Katie had felt Luke's eyes on her most of the night and the look of admiration on his face right now made her uneasy. "I'm hardly an expert."

"You know more than a thing or two about kitchens, Katie. Admit it."

Mason spoke up. "She's right, Katie."

"Just take the compliment," Drea said, grinning.

Katie nodded, giving in. "O…kay, if you insist."

Luke laughed and she eyed him carefully. "What's so funny?"

His lips went tight and he shook his head. "Nothin'."

She was afraid he would say she was cute or something equally as revealing, so she dropped it. But she knew his laugh now and when it was aimed at her.

Dessert and coffee were served. The pastries, pies and cakes were beautiful, but Katie had barely eaten her dinner so the thought of dessert didn't sit well. Beef Wellington had sounded good on the menu, but as soon as the dish arrived, Katie had lost her appetite. She'd been feeling queasy lately, and for good reason. She'd married the enemy and the nightmare was continuing. She felt out of control, restless and confused about her feelings for Luke.

"I'll sit this one out," she said politely.

"Too much cupcake sampling at the bakery?" Drea asked.

"Uh, yeah. I'm really full," she said, and Drea gave her a look. She was astute enough not to ask her what was wrong, but she had no doubt her friend would be questioning her about it later on. "But you go on. Enjoy. Everything looks delicious."

After dessert, Mason and Drea took to the dance floor again. Her friend knew enough not to try to coax her out there with Luke. Thank goodness.

She glanced at her watch and noted the time. "Luke, it's after nine."

"Yeah," he said. "I know. You've been checking your watch every five minutes since we got here."

"I have not."

"You have." He ran his hand down his face in his classic frustrated move and it irritated her no end.

"Lucas Boone, exactly what is it you want from me?"

That stumped him for a second. He blinked his eyes and then stared at her. "You would be surprised."

Her heart started racing. "Would I?"

"I have absolutely no doubt you would, so let's drop it." He rose. "Grab your purse. I'll take you home now."

They waited until the dance ended to say goodbye to Drea and Mason. "Thank you for this evening, it was wonderful," Katie said.

"I'm glad you enjoyed it," Mason answered.

She hugged Drea goodbye, too, and then she and Luke were off.

The drive home was quiet, uncharacteristically so. Luke didn't spare her a word or a glance and she felt the tension down to her toes. "Are you mad at me?" she asked.

He inhaled a breath and shook his head. "No."

"Is that all you're going to say?"

"Yep. That's all." He kept his gaze trained on the road.

She folded her arms around her middle, and her stomach knotted up. She'd almost forgotten how unsettled it felt. It was all this stress, and she was put off that Luke, regardless of his denial, was angry with her.

If anyone had a right to be angry, it was her. "Well, maybe I'm mad at you."

"What?" This time he did take his eyes off the road. He had an incredulous look on his face. "I'm not the one who spoiled the evening for Mason and Drea. They were trying to do a nice thing. And you refused to participate."

"I didn't refuse to participate. I just didn't want to… be with you. And for some reason, you don't seem to understand that."

"Oh, I get it all right. But couldn't you have shown some appreciation to my brother and Drea? You wouldn't dance, wouldn't eat. Why was that, *wife*?"

He said that just to rub salt in her wound. "Don't be an ass, Luke. I could never be your wife. And you know darn well I didn't spoil anything."

Her belly clenched and her face pulled tight as she absorbed the pain. "Uh." She glanced out the window, hiding her discomfort, hoping Luke wouldn't catch on.

"What's wrong?"

"Nothing." She wouldn't look at him.

Luke steered the car onto the side of the road and parked along the highway.

"What are you doing?" she asked, breathless.

"What's wrong with you?"

"I told you, nothing is wrong with me." Once again, her stomach rolled and she bit her lip. She didn't want to get sick in front of him. They were in semidarkness, the moonlight casting them in shadows. "But I would appreciate it if you took me home."

"Can we just talk a minute?" he asked.

"I'm not feeling well, okay? It's all this stress. I'm

worried sick about my mother and sister finding out about…about what happened. And being with you makes me go a little nutty."

"Katie," he said, his voice ultra-soft now. "I'm sorry you're not feeling well. Why didn't you say something before?"

"I didn't want to ruin the evening. But according to you, I'm guilty of that, too."

"Katie," he whispered. "I was just being—"

"A jerk?"

"Okay," he said, defeat in his voice. "I was a jerk. Of course you didn't spoil anything. So I make you nutty? Do you hate me that much?"

"Luke, I don't hate you. I never did. Maybe my problem is that… I like you. And it's impossible."

"You like me?" His voice rose, filled with hope.

"Luke, we've been… Well, you know. I keep asking myself why I let that happen. True, it was grief over Snow, but—"

"How much do you like me?"

He was crazy to think anything could ever come of the two of them, yet he was asking as if there was a chance. "Not enough to destroy my sister and hurt my mother." Her stomach cramped and she put her hand on it. "Oh."

"Katie?"

"Luke, please, take me home."

Concern entered his eyes. "Okay, just sit back and try to relax. I'll get you home quickly, sweetheart."

She wasn't his sweetheart. She wasn't his anything, and she hoped this little talk would convince him of that.

A short time later, he pulled up in front of the bakery. "Hold on a second," he said and got out of the car to open the door for her. He took her hand and helped her out.

"Thanks for the ride." She turned away from him, but he didn't release her hand.

"I'll make sure you get in safely."

The front door was ten feet away. "I'll be fine."

"I'll walk you," he said stubbornly and he walked beside her as she made her way to the front of the bakery.

She unlocked the door and took a step inside.

"Katie?"

"What?" She turned to him.

His eyes were soft on her, his expression etched in concern. "Are you feeling any better?"

"A little."

He tipped her chin up and planted a sweet tender kiss to her lips. It instantly warmed her insides, soothing her. "Get some rest. I'll check on you tomorrow."

Before she could say "Don't," he had turned away and hopped into his car. A dreamy feeling flowed through her body as if she was floating.

Until she realized that Luke had just kissed her on the public street.

And someone might have seen them.

She took a peek, noting the sidewalks were empty, and there were no cars in sight, yet her belly twisted up again. And all feelings of warmth quickly evaporated.

Early the next morning, Luke pulled up in front of the bakery, wondering if he was making a mistake by showing up here. He had Katie on the brain, and just remembering how she'd looked in that sexy gown last night, how delicious her lips tasted when he'd given her a goodbye kiss, gave him some hope that she wouldn't mind him checking in on her.

She'd admitted she liked him. He'd been floored hearing those words come out of her mouth. It was more than he'd expected, more than he'd thought possible. It was a start. Keeping away from her for the past five years had been hard on him, but Las Vegas had changed all that.

He got out of the car and entered the bakery, disappointed to see her assistant behind the counter helping customers. He was hit with a knot of apprehension. Was Katie still feeling poorly?

And just then she walked out of the kitchen and into the bakery. They made eye contact. There was a spark in her eyes, a light that she quickly extinguished. But he'd seen it and she couldn't deny that for that one second, she'd been happy to see him.

He took a seat in a café chair and waited, watching Katie and Lori efficiently handle the morning rush. Finally, once the crowded bakery thinned out, Katie walked over to him. "I hope you're here to give me news...about you know what," she whispered.

She was speaking about the divorce.

"No change on that, I'm afraid."

She pursed her lips. "Then why are you here?"

He shrugged. "For coffee."

She tapped her foot. "Can I get you anything else?"

"Just coffee for now."

She hesitated. "Don't you have a coffee cart at Boone Inc.?"

"We do, but as you can see, I'm not at Boone Inc. at the moment. I'm here."

She sighed. "I'll get it for you." She turned to leave.

"Katie," he said firmly.

She gave him a deadpan look.

"How are you feeling?"

"I'm fine. Now will you go?"

"Coffee, please."

She gave her head a shake and left only to return a moments later holding a steaming cup of coffee. "Here you go." She set the cup in front of him.

"Sit with me."

"I can't, I'm working."

"Just for a minute." He pointed around the shop. "The place has emptied out."

"Only if you promise to leave as soon as you're through."

"Fine."

She sat down facing him, and once up close, he noticed the fatigue on her face and how her eyes were rimmed with red. She'd been moving slowly around the bakery. "How are you feeling?"

"I feel…good."

She was lying. "Don't take this the wrong way, but you look sluggish this morning."

"What every girl wants to hear. Thank you for that."

He shook his head. The woman was constantly sparring with him. Today, it wasn't cute or funny. "How's your stomach?"

"Luke, you don't have to check up on me. I'm perfectly capable of taking care of myself. So please, have your coffee and leave."

"Is that any way to speak to a customer? One you actually like."

She sighed. "Luke, I'm beginning to regret telling you that."

"Just for the record. I like you, too. A lot."

"Shh." She glanced at the door.

What was she so afraid of? Was she expecting to see her sister or mother walk in this morning? Was that it? Diana and Shelly had to know he and Katie had wedding business to discuss. They were both helping Aunt Lottie put on the bridal shower for Drea and Mason. Luke and Katie had been thrown together lately and it shouldn't be a crime that the two of them spent some time together.

He sipped his coffee. "Mmm, perfect."

"I'll tell Lori you enjoyed it. She makes a mean cup."

"So, I'll see you at the bridal shower on Saturday. Are we all set for that?"

"I am. I'm making the cake and helping with some of the activities."

"I'm good on my end, too." He actually wasn't asked to do much, just help the day of the shower behind the scenes. "I can pick you up and bring you out to the ranch."

"That's silly. You live at the ranch. You don't need to come all the way out here to pick me up. I'll manage."

She was good at shooting him down.

"I am sorry, you know," he said. "I don't like being the source of your stress. But I can't do anything about that right now."

"I'll…try to remember that. So no more sudden visits to the shop?"

"I can't promise that. I might have a craving."

Katie gave him a hard stare.

"For a cupcake."

She nibbled on her lip, trying to keep from saying something. Whatever it was, he was sure he didn't want to hear it. He finished his drink, then rose and reached out to help her up, but she ignored his outstretched hand.

"Just try to rest. Feel better, Katie."

The genuine concern in his voice caused a momentary tug in her heart. The truth was, she hadn't had anyone care about her this way in a long time. And it felt sort of nice. This was what she'd longed for, what she'd revealed to Luke in Las Vegas. She wanted more out of life. She wanted a partner, someone to share things with. She'd neglected that part of her life to make the bakery a success. Now, she had a thriving business, but no one to share it with.

Perhaps she should start dating again.

And then she remembered…she couldn't date anyone.

She was married to Lucas Boone.

Three days later, Lottie opened the front door of the ranch house at Rising Springs to face Drew MacDonald. He was the last person she was expecting this morning and her heart did a little flip seeing him looking so handsome with a salt-and-pepper beard, his graying, windswept hair and his workout clothes the same shade of jade green as his Irish eyes.

It had been awkward between them lately but she wanted to rectify that. They were all going to be family as soon as Mason and Drea, Drew's daughter, were married. And this weekend, Lottie was throwing the two lovebirds a couples bridal shower.

"Hi, Drew. I didn't expect to see you this morning."

Suddenly, she remembered what she must look like. She was cooking up a storm, baking apple cobbler and cookies for her nephews. Not only were her clothes a mess, but she probably had flour on her face and in her hair.

"I didn't come to see you."

"Oh."

"I mean, I'm happy to see you and all, but Luke asked me to stop by some time this morning. He needs a bit of advice about a company I used to deal with. Anyway, I decided to stop by after my walk."

"I see. I'm glad you're still taking walks, Drew."

"I enjoy it. But I sure liked it better when I had a walking partner." He gave her a direct look.

Warmth rushed up her cheeks. The man could always make her blush. "You need that much motivation?"

"No, ma'am. Just liked the company." And before she could react, he took a deep breath. "Something smells awfully good in here."

"I'm baking, in case you can't tell." She gestured to her smudged clothes. "Apple cobbler and lemon supreme cookies. I'll send some home for you and Drea."

"Thanks. I'd never refuse any of your baking, Lottie.

Though I'd probably have to walk farther every day just to burn off the calories."

"I don't think apple cobbler would do you any harm. You're, uh, looking fit these days."

They stared at each other for a few beats of a minute. "Well, if Luke's home, maybe I could see him now?"

"Oh, right. Sure, he's in the office. You know where it is. Go on in."

"Thanks. Oh, and it was nice talking to you this morning."

"Same here, Drew."

After he turned and walked down the hallway, she smiled. It seemed they could have a civil conversation if they put their mind to it. She went back to baking and thinking about Drew, her heart lighter than it had been in a long while.

An hour later, she came downstairs after taking a quick shower and changing her clothes. She wore a soft pink bell sleeve blouse. It worked well with her rosy complexion, and silly her, she found herself dressing to impress. She gave a quick knock on the office door and then entered.

Luke was sitting in front of his laptop computer, Drew nowhere in sight. "Hi, Aunt Lottie. What's up?"

"Oh, I thought you were having a meeting with Drew?"

"I was. He left a little bit ago." Luke grinned. "Don't you look pretty today. I thought you were baking."

"I was and I'm finished now. I meant to send Drew home with some cobbler and cookies for Drea."

"Just for Drea?" he asked, his mouth twitching.

She chuckled. She'd been caught. "Well, for both of them."

"So, what's stopping you? Take it over to them. I'm sure they'd appreciate it."

"You think so?"

"I know so. Drew loves his sweets."

"That is true." She mulled it over for half a second. She hadn't gotten all dressed up for nothing. "Okay, I think I will."

Luke smiled the smile of a matchmaker. The only thing missing was him rubbing his hands together gleefully. "Good idea."

And a few minutes later Lottie was set with a canvas tote containing the lemon cookies and a covered dish of still warm cobbler. She took off on foot; the extra bit of exercise today would do her good. Her heart was aflutter, thinking about Drew and how much he was beginning to mean to her.

As she approached the MacDonald cottage, Drew opened his front door and out stepped a pretty, dark-haired woman she'd never seen before. The two embraced in a passionate hug that lasted far too long. And then the woman took his face in her hands and kissed him right smack on the mouth.

Shocked, Lottie froze for a moment, not believing what she was seeing. She stood on the road, bag in hand, ready to make nice with Drew, and now she was hit with raw pangs of jealousy. She couldn't watch any longer. She turned on her heels and made fast tracks away from the cottage before Drew could see her.

Goodness, what an idiot she was. Had she been naive

to think that Drew didn't have other options when it came to women? He'd straightened himself out, was ruggedly handsome and had a good heart, for the most part. She'd always thought of him as hers in an odd sort of way. Had he led her on all these years? Or had she been blind to his needs?

Either way, she was roaring mad at him and his sweet-talking ways.

As her anger raged, she picked up her pace, walking as fast as her legs would take her. Running from the hurt, from the loss, from the betrayal as tears trickled down her face.

Five

"I'm here, Mama," Katie called as she unlocked the door and entered her mother's house Thursday afternoon.

She didn't find her right away. But soon Shelly appeared, coming in through the sliding back door. "Mom's in the backyard, getting some fresh air."

"That's a good idea. It's a beautiful afternoon. How're you doing, sis? Staying for dinner?"

"No, sorry. I hope you're okay with making Mom dinner without me. I'm… I'm going to a seminar tonight. It includes dinner."

"That's no problem, but another seminar? You know what they say, too much work and not enough play…"

Shelly smiled. "If I'm dull, then I'm dull. I happen to love my work."

"I get it. I love my work, too." Then Katie grinned. "Is a certain Dr. Moore going to this event?"

"Take that grin off your face, brat. And actually Dr. Moore is giving the seminar, part two of his Cardiology in the Twenty-first Century lecture. So of course he's going to be there."

"Now the evening's sounding more interesting." Katie smiled again.

Her sister picked up a pillow and tossed it at her, just like when they were kids. Katie was too fast for her. "You missed me."

"Only because I wasn't really trying."

There was a breezy lightness to Shelly tonight that she hoped would continue.

"So, Katie, any chance we can go shopping with Mom on Saturday? I have the day off and I thought it'd be nice to get her out of the house. You know, have a girls' day."

"Oh, that's a great idea, but I can't do it Saturday. It's Drea and Mason's bridal shower."

Shelly's perpetual frown reappeared. So much for light and breezy. "Oh, right. That's if Mason decides to show up for it. Boones are notorious for disappointing their fiancées."

"Shel, give it a rest, okay? Drea's crazy about him."

"Yeah, well, I was crazy about Luke and look how that turned out. I mean, he was an amazing boyfriend and fiancée until he wasn't."

"I know it hurt you, but you can't change the past," Katie said, trying to get through to her sister. Trying to ease her own conscience, too.

"I know that. But I also know I can't suppress my emotions."

"But you're suppressing living your life."

Shelly gave her head a tilt. "You really think so?"

"I absolutely do. You have a lot to offer someone. You should be open to that."

"Well, it's not as if anyone's busting down the door to get to me."

"How about you taking a chance. Walk out the door and find what you're looking for."

"I'm...scared."

Katie winced. It was hard seeing her big sister admit that. She took Shelly's hands in hers and squeezed. "Shel, you're strong enough to deal with anything that comes your way. You're a fantastic person, a wonderful nurse. You make people feel better, you care. People look up to you, they value your judgment. Never doubt that. I think that you'll find what you're looking for if you give yourself a chance."

Shelly drew a breath. "Maybe." She nodded. "I'll try. And thanks, sis. You're the best."

The conversation made Katie ache inside for the pain her sister had gone through. Hearing her admit that she'd been crazy about Luke was like a dagger to her heart.

Because Katie was starting to have real feelings for Luke.

And they were getting stronger every day.

Saturday morning, Katie rose extra early to get a head start on baking so she'd have enough time to put the finishing touches on the bridal shower cake. Though cakes weren't her specialty, she knew enough about them to design a one-of-a-kind cake for Drea and Mason that resembled the home they were building on Rising Springs land. It took a great deal of thought, but the cake when finished would be spectacular.

Halfway through the decorating, fatigue set in, and she took a seat to rest. She'd been stressed out lately, and for good reason, but she'd never felt so tired before. Her mother told her she was taking on too much, that she needed extra help running the bakery, but Katie didn't think that was it.

"You look as green as this pistachio icing," Lori said, picking up a freshly frosted tray of cupcakes. "Are you feeling poorly?"

"I think I'm just tired. I worked hard on the cake last night and didn't get much sleep. I probably should've closed the shop today, so I could concentrate on Drea's shower."

"Why don't you go up to your apartment and get some rest? I'll finish up with the cupcakes, so you can be fresh for the bridal shower."

Normally, Katie wouldn't think of it, but her tummy was aching, the same queasy feeling she'd been having for days now. "I'll go up for an hour if you don't mind."

"Go, I've got things covered here."

"I have no doubt. You could run this bakery with your eyes closed. I'll be back soon."

"Take your time," Lori said.

"Thanks." Katie climbed the stairs to her apartment and once inside, her stomach cramped tight and she couldn't fight the nausea. "Oh no." Her hand on her belly, she dashed to the bathroom and made it just in time. When she was through, she sat down on the tile floor next to the toilet until her tummy settled down.

Where had that come from? She thought back to what she'd eaten these past few days but nothing struck her as odd. Could it be stress and fatigue causing such a disruption to her health?

She rose and took a shower, then tucked herself into bed. She'd rest for just a few minutes and then get up to put the finishing touches on the cake.

The sound of birds tweeting broke into her sleep. Katie opened her eyes and listened again. Those weren't real birds, it was her cell phone chirping. She grabbed it off the nightstand. Her eyes widened when she saw the time and she jolted out of bed, panicked. It was nine o'clock! She was supposed to be at the ranch in half an hour. The shower was starting at noon.

The text read, Drea's sending me to pick you up. Stay put.

It was from Luke.

Oh God. She was late. She took a few minutes to dress and comb her hair and then raced downstairs. "Lori, I'm so sorry," she called out. She didn't have time to deal with Luke coming to get her. Actually, with the way she was feeling, she really could use his help.

"Hey, no problem," Lori said, coming into the work area. "It's slow right now, but I was beginning to worry. Are you feeling better?"

Gosh, she didn't have time to feel bad. She had to finish the cake and get to Rising Springs. "Yes, I'm better.

The rest did me a world of good but I've got to finish the cake. Should only take a few minutes."

Katie pulled the cake out of the fridge and spent the next twenty minutes piping the perimeter and adding the names. When all was said and done, the two-tiered cake looked like a picture of serenity and love.

"There," she said, with a heavy dose of pride and relief.

"It's beautiful." Luke had sneaked up beside her. She hadn't heard him enter but she appreciated the compliment.

"Thanks."

"A lot of work?"

"Yes," she replied. "But worth the effort."

"Funny, that's how I feel about you."

Katie turned to find a twinkle in his eye. "Luke."

He grinned. "C'mon. Let's get our butts to the house before the shower starts without us."

"You really didn't have to come."

"Drea insisted, and who am I to argue with my future sister?"

"Riiiight."

She wouldn't tell him she was glad he'd come to the rescue, that she had been sluggish lately and she hoped once they settled their "marriage" problem, her tummy aches would disappear.

Luke had driven with extra caution while Katie sat in the back seat of his roomy SUV with the double-tiered cake beside her. And now, thanks to Luke carefully carrying it inside, the cake sat on the kitchen counter, ready to be revealed once the shower began.

As Katie put up snow-white paper wedding bells along the perimeter of the spacious patio overhang, Luke held the ladder for her, watching her carefully. "You sure you don't want me to do that?" he asked her, for the second time.

"Not at all. These have to be spaced just right and hung a certain way."

"And a mere man can't figure it out?"

She laughed. She was having fun decorating for her best friend's shower and she didn't want anyone to take the joy away. "I think not."

"That's okay, I'm enjoying the view from down here anyway."

Katie immediately grabbed at the back of her dress, making sure she was well covered. The dress was tight enough to cling to her legs. But she noticed it was fitting a little more snugly around her waist than she'd remembered. She had to stop eating her own cupcakes. "You can't see anything, Luke, so stop teasing."

"Everything I do see, I like."

She gave him a look. "Shh."

"I meant the decorations are looking real pretty. Everyone's doing a great job."

She shook her head at him. He was so full of it. But in a sweet way that made her…nutty.

From her vantage point on the ladder, everyone was pitching in and doing a great job. Risk and April were arranging the table flowers. April was an expert at staging homes so her expertise was spot on. The next home she would permanently stage would be at Canyon Lake Lodge, the old manor that Risk had bought for them to live in once they renovated it. The two were going to run the lodge together.

Drea and Mason were locked in an embrace watching the lily pads they'd set afloat in the pool drift off. Their happiness was contagious. Katie could be happy for them, and for this day. It was a dream come true for Drea, who'd been through so much in the past.

"Okay," Katie said, draping the last of the wedding bells. "I think I'm done."

She lowered herself down from the ladder and was hit with a bout of dizziness. Her head swam for a moment and Luke was right there, taking her hands, staring into her eyes. "Katie?"

"Whoa," she said. "That was weird."

"What happened?"

"Nothing." She gave her head a gentle shake. "I think I came down the ladder too fast. Got a little light-headed. I'm fine now."

He stepped closer to her. "Are you sure?"

"Yes," she said automatically. She stepped back from him, breaking their connection. She didn't want him worrying over her. She didn't want to see concern on his face or hear it in his voice. It was all too confusing.

Lottie approached with a gracious smile. "Katie, the cake is amazing. I can't wait for the guests to see it. We'll bring it out soon to show off your beautiful work."

"Thanks, Lottie. I'm—"

"She worked hard on it, Aunt Lottie." There was

possessive pride in Luke's voice that had Lottie darting inquisitive glances between them.

"I can see that."

"It was a labor of love," Katie said.

Lottie patted her hand. "I bet you have a lot of love to give, Katie."

"I'm sort of married, uh..." She hesitated when Luke's eyes went shockingly wide. "To my job. I mean, right now I'm concentrating on the bakery. I haven't had time for anything else," she said quietly.

"Well, when you find the right one, you'll know it. There's no rush."

Katie nodded. "I agree. No rush at all."

Drew walked up and smiled at everyone. "Katie, I just saw the cake. You've outdone yourself."

"Thank you."

"I bet it tastes as good as it looks."

"Hope so."

"Drew's got a sweet tooth," Luke said good-naturedly. "I bet you enjoyed Aunt Lottie's cobbler the other day, too. Did you leave any crumbs for Drea?"

Drew's brows furrowed. "Cobbler? If you mean the day I stopped by to see you, Luke, I left your place before getting a chance to dig in."

"But she brought you some that day, didn't you, Aunt Lottie?"

Luke's aunt bit her lip and shook her head. "No, I never made it over."

She didn't give Drew a glance, and her expression was tight. After that, Lottie excused herself to speak with the caterer and Drew walked off in the other direction. Katie thought for sure something was up between the two of them.

She looked at the string and tape and scissors she'd left lying around. "Okay, well, I'd better clean up my mess. The guests will be arriving soon."

"I'll help," Luke said.

Katie couldn't shake the guy. He turned up beside her at every turn. It made mush of her nerves because she was getting used to him being around. She scooped up her mess before Luke could grab anything. "I've got this," she said. "But Mason might need your help. You should check with him."

"In other words, you want me to get lost."

She smiled.

And Luke took the hint. "I'll see you later."

"Okay," she said brightly and once he walked off, Katie entered the house and took a seat in the kitchen. Her tummy was still a bit unsettled and her energy was sapped.

She couldn't wait for the shower to begin and end. All she could think about was getting back into bed and sleeping.

Katie squinted into the bright May sunshine as she stepped out into the Boones' beautifully groomed backyard that they'd spent hours decorating. Everything had turned out perfectly. Drea's dream of true love and marriage was coming true.

The guests filed in as music played over hidden speakers. She watched as groups mingled and enjoyed appetizers and drank wine. Some of the girls in attendance were her friends, too, many of them either married, engaged or escorted by a boyfriend. She sighed and put on a happy face to mingle as well and catch up on their news.

Once the luncheon was served, everyone took their seats. Katie sat at the Boone table. Everyone was paired off with their counterparts, leaving her sitting next to Luke. Funny how it always worked out that way.

He seemed perfectly content with the arrangements and all she could do was smile and have a good time, for Drea's sake. Most of the guests played a silly game of who knew the bride and groom the best, and Katie ended up winning the bride half of the game.

Drea and Mason opened their gifts, and then Katie was asked to cut their cake, but not before a dozen pictures were taken of it. Katie was showered with compliments, which gave her spirit a lift. She found herself smiling and laughing a lot throughout the day.

"I'm glad to see you so happy," Luke whispered in her ear as they sipped coffee.

"I'm happy for Drea."

"Me, too. For Mason. The guy's gaga over his fiancée."

"As well he should be. Drea is awesome."

"So are—"

She put a finger to his lips to quiet him, and then realized what she'd done and quickly removed it, but not before a few heads turned her way. Oh God, had they seen her trying to silence his compliment?

Luke didn't let it faze him. He bit into a forkful of cake. "This is delicious."

She shot him a warning look, but that never seemed to work with him. "Thanks."

As the shower was winding down, Katie decided to remove herself from his presence. "Excuse me. I'm needed in the kitchen, and no, I don't need any help."

She escaped him and entered the kitchen, offering to help, but Lottie shoed her away. "You've done enough. The staff will take care of cleanup. Honestly, I think that's the best marble cake I've ever eaten. It's beautiful on the inside and out. You're a genius."

Drew walked into the kitchen and added, "That you are, Katie girl. I had seconds and would go back for thirds if I was twenty years younger."

Lottie feigned a smile and turned her back on him.

"Thank you both," Katie said. "Lottie, if you really don't need my help, I'll go outside and talk to Drea."

"Good idea," Lottie said. "Go have fun. I'll be out in a second."

Lottie watched Katie leave and then turned to Drew. "Honestly, I don't need any help here. You should go back outside, too."

"Kicking me out?" His mouth quirked up.

Lottie sighed. "No, you can stay or you can go. Do whatever you want, Drew."

Drew frowned. "Lottie, what the hell is wrong with you? You haven't spoken to me all day. Did I do something wrong, again?"

He was annoyed at her? Did he think she was a fool? The image of Drew kissing that woman on his porch flashed in her mind and anger roiled in her stomach.

It was time to confront him. There was no other way. "Not at all. I mean, kissing a woman behind my back isn't wrong. Not if you read from the book of Drew Mac-Donald."

"What are you talking about?"

"I saw you, Drew. The other day, I was bringing you a dish of cobbler and I… I saw a woman coming out of your house. You two were very cozy. I guess I've been mistaken about the two of us. There is no us."

Drew's green eyes sparked and she couldn't tell what he was thinking. "There is no us?" He took her hand and tugged her close. "Lady, you have no idea."

Then he cupped her face in his hands and laid a kiss on her lips. Her heart fluttered and her mind dizzied as delicious sensations sped through her system. She kissed him back, trying to keep pace with his passion, his ardor.

She couldn't seem to get enough of him, and he must've been feeling the same way. He pulled her into his arms and she went willingly. His kisses went deeper, longer and nothing, nothing she'd experienced in this world had ever felt better. "Drew," she murmured.

He kissed her again, the melding of their mouths seamless and perfect.

Then he broke away and her eyes popped open. She stared at him and he said with a rasp, "Now, tell me there is no us."

"But the woman?"

"I'm her AA sponsor and she needed a one-on-one talk. Whatever you saw was gratitude. *She* kissed me and I set her straight right after that. My goodness, Lottie, she's half my age."

"So, you're not—"

"After the way we just kissed, you have to ask?"

Then he turned his back on her and walked outside. She touched a finger to her mouth, his taste still tingling on her lips.

On the drive home after the shower, Luke kept glancing at Katie. She sat in the passenger seat of his car, struggling to keep her eyes open as she laid her head against the headrest. Snuggled into her jacket, she looked warm and cozy and so peaceful, her body sinking into the contours of the seat.

He tried not to utter a sound as he drove along the quiet road, and before too long, she fell asleep. Luke drove on, feeling the rightness of this moment in his bones. He and Katie. There was no other woman in the world for him and as each day passed, the feeling grew stronger and stronger.

While she was hoping for a quick divorce, he was stalling…perhaps wrongfully so, but all those years while he was in Afghanistan serving his country, he'd felt hollow and empty inside. It was the worst feeling in the world, that aloneness, that feeling that aside from his brothers, there was no one waiting for him back home. Now, he had what he'd always wanted. It would be hard giving it up.

He could tell she was bone tired by the way she was huddled between the seat and the window, her breaths as noisy as they were weary.

Katie was a force, a dynamo in a very understated way. She'd made Katie's Kupcakes a success. And all the while, she'd continued supporting Red Barrel, donating her time and energy to neglected and abandoned horses. She was a great friend, a wonderful daughter and an ultra-loyal sister.

Luke sighed. He wanted to reach out and hold her hand, but that might wake her. That might put her on alert and it was the last thing he wanted, to make her wary, to have her erect walls that would keep him out. No, he was content to have her near him, to watch her sleep. Too soon, he would have to part ways with her.

Once they reached her street, Luke steered his car to the back door of her shop and parked. She'd want him to use discretion so the people strolling along the sidewalk wouldn't see him trying to get a sleepy Katie out of his car.

He didn't give two figs about being seen with her, so this he did for her.

"Sweetheart," he said gently, taking her hand trying to rouse her.

She didn't wake readily, only curled deeper into the comfort of her jacket.

"Katie, honey, you're home. You need to wake up."

She mumbled something incoherently and continued to sleep.

"Okay," he said on a whisper. "Looks like you need Prince Charming, only I don't see him anywhere around here."

He smirked at his bad joke and then got out of the car. When he opened her passenger side door, he hoped the cooler air would jostle her awake. When that didn't happen, he scooped her up in his arms, taking her hand-bag along with him.

"Luke," she breathed out and the sound of her sultry voice nearly did him in. His wholesome Katie was a very sexy temptation.

"I've got you."

He managed to dig the keys out of her purse, and once inside the bakery, he climbed the stairs to her apartment. Sleep tousled and still drowsy, she was light in his arms and relaxed enough to lie against his chest as he opened her apartment door. He carried her inside and wanted so much to deposit her onto her bed and lie down next to her.

Once in her living room, he set her on her feet and held on as she gained her footing. "Katie?"

She opened her eyes and gazed up at him. "Sorry. I was just so tired. I don't know why… I've never been that tired before."

Touching her cheek, Luke brushed a honey blond strand of hair off her face. "It's not a problem," he said quietly. "You've had a lot on your plate, sweetheart."

"I guess that must be it." The apartment was cool and dark and Katie looked so tempting, so soft. "Did I sleep all the way home?"

"Not all the way."

She covered her face with her hands. "Oh gosh. I'm so embarrassed. You're always seeing me at my worst."

"That's an impossibility, Katie."

"Luke," she warned, but with a smile on her face.

Yeah, he knew the drill. She was constantly giving him warnings. Yet Katie didn't know how hard it was standing this close to her while she looked so damn tousled and sexy. She had no idea how hard it was for him to say good-night when he was legally married to her. He summoned up his willpower. "I'd better get going. Let you get some rest."

Was that a twinge of disappointment in her eyes? "It's probably for the best."

"Yeah," he said, hating to go. He touched a finger to her cheek and then kissed her there, softly, tenderly. "Good night then." He turned away from her, leaving her looking a little bit lost in the middle of the room.

When he was halfway to the door, she called to him. "Luke?"

He spun on his heels and faced her.

She took a big swallow. "Don't go."

Oh God. He drew breath into his lungs and approached her. "Why?"

"I mean you can go if you want to, but I'm just saying I'm not as tired now and if you'd like to stay for coffee or a drink, that would be nice. But you don't have to, you can always—"

"I'll stay."

"You will?"

He nodded. She had no idea how much he'd wanted to hear those words.

"But if I do, I'd want—"

"I, uh, sort of know what you want, Luke." She squeezed her eyes closed briefly.

He scratched his head. She was just so adorable. "I was going to say I'd want a cupcake with that coffee. If it's not too much trouble."

A look of relief swept over her face. "No, not at all. I'm your go-to for all things cupcake."

His go-to for all things, period.

"Just kick me out when you want me to leave," he said. They'd lingered after the bridal shower, Katie going gaga over Drea's gifts and talk of the wedding, while he had beers with both of his brothers, but it was still early in the evening.

She chuckled. "Don't worry. I will."

He didn't want to dwell on how easy it was for her to reject him, time and again. "So, are you always this peppy after a long nap?"

"I don't know. I usually don't take naps," she said as she walked into the kitchen and flipped on the light. She arranged half a dozen mouthwatering cupcakes on a dish and put them on the table, then began making coffee. "Have a seat."

Luke opted not to sit at the table. He leaned against the kitchen counter, watching her work. It smelled good in her kitchen, like sugar and warmth. "I plan on going to the rescue tomorrow. Haven't been back since Snow passed."

"Neither have I," she admitted. She stopped pouring ground beans into the coffee maker and bit her lip. "It's gonna be hard going back."

"Yeah. But there are so many other horses who need attention. After the wedding, I'm going to look into raising funds for Red Barrel. I've already spoken to Wes about it. They could use more financial support."

"It's a good idea, but I know your family—you, mostly—have been donating on a regular basis."

"How do you know that?"

"I hear things and that's all I'm going to say."

"You like keeping secrets, is that it?"

Her eyes grew as round as the cupcakes on the platter. "I certainly do not. I'm a very honest person and I hate secrets. You're the one making anonymous donations to the rescue and secretly marrying the first girl too drunk to know better." She blinked several times.

"First of all, sweetheart, it's not a crime to make a private donation once in a while. And second of all, you're not the first girl."

"Oh."

"You're the only girl."

She met his eyes and whispered, "Don't, Luke."

"Why'd you really invite me in tonight? And I want the honest truth."

She put her chin up, as if refusing to answer, but he stared at her for a long time and then her eyes fluttered and finally she admitted, "I get lonely…sometimes."

His heart pulled tight and he touched a finger to her cheek, the skin smooth and soft there. "You don't ever have to be, not when I'm around."

She took a hard swallow, her eyes filled with regret. He hated seeing her looking so torn and scared. He couldn't have her afraid of him. She had to know he was her safe space. Leaning against the counter, he took her hand and brought her into the cradle of his arms. Her body pressed against his and all his willpower dashed out the window. *Oh man.*

"You don't have to say those things," she said quietly. "You're not really my husband."

"We have a marriage license to prove it," he said, kissing her forehead.

"It's just paper. It's not real."

"It's not just paper, sweetheart. And that's why you're fighting it so much."

"We've had this argument before," she said softly.

"Let's not have it again." And then he brushed his lips over hers and made love to her mouth until the coffeepot sizzled and the cupcakes were long forgotten.

Katie didn't want to have this uncanny, impossible attraction to Lucas Boone. Her brain was telling her no, no, no, while all other parts of her body screamed out yes. She'd never been in this kind of dilemma before. Usually she'd follow reason, but Luke had turned her rational thinking upside down.

Now, after abandoning the coffee and cupcakes, both stood naked and aroused in her bedroom facing each other. It was a blur how quickly they'd shed their clothes and wound up in here. One earthquake of a kiss was all it had taken. They were cast mostly in shadow with only a glimmer of moonlight peeking in through the shutters.

"I want to know all of you," Luke said, taking her hand and kissing the inside of her palm. "I want you to know all of me, too."

Katie drew breath into her lungs. It seemed the harder she pushed him away, the more she thought about him, the more she wanted him. And now she was giving in to her true feelings, too tired to fight them any longer.

She knew what he wanted and as she touched him, caressed him, she could only relish his groans of pleasure, his quick breaths. It was too good, too delicious, the sensations wrapping them both up causing heat to climb rapidly.

And when she was through pleasuring him, he kissed her long and hard and then moved her onto the bed and returned the favor.

She was out of her mind with one burning hot sensation after another. He was a master with his mouth, his hands. He knew not only where to touch her, but how to touch her, making her feel worshipped and treasured. His kisses made her pulse with lust and need. Then when his broad, powerful body covered hers, sheathed in protection and moving deep inside her thrust after thrust, she cried out his name and climaxed to the highest peak.

It was beautiful. It was perfectly amazing. And scary as hell.

Minutes later, Luke tucked her close, spooning her, his breath soft on her neck. He reached around to cup her breast with one hand and fondle her with his masterful fingers.

"You're beautiful this way," he said, kissing her shoulder.

"What way?" she asked, smiling. She was still blissfully coming down from her release.

"Naked."

She laughed.

He kissed her again. "But I also like it when you're relaxed like this."

"Hmm. We do well like this," Katie admitted.

"Excuse me, did I just hear you say you think we're good together?"

"I wouldn't go that…far. Oh." He strummed his thumb over her nipple, sending immediate heat down to her belly. He was relentless, toying with her body, his hand stroking over places that could make her weep in pleasure.

"You wouldn't?" He brought his mouth to her shoulder and kissed her again and again. She squeezed her eyes tight. "Tell the truth."

"We can't be…together, Luke."

"Seems like we are together, sweetheart. And it's no use trying to deny it."

She turned to face him. She had to keep her resolve firm or they'd all live to regret it. "Luke, let's not argue about this. Not tonight. Can we change the subject?"

He paused, masking his feelings with a blank stare, which was fine with her. She didn't want to delve too deeply into his emotions. Or hers, for that matter. "What would you like to talk about?"

She turned onto her back and focused on the delicate patterns created by moonlight on the ceiling. "How about your father?"

"My father?" She'd surprised him, but she'd always been curious about Henry Boone. He'd been legendary, but she was curious about something that was said about him.

"Yes," she said. "He had a reputation for being sort of a… Well, there's no other way to say this. It was rumored he was quite ruthless in business."

"FAST FIVE" READER SURVEY

Your participation entitles you to:
* ✳ 4 Thank-You Gifts Worth Over $20!

Complete the survey in minutes.

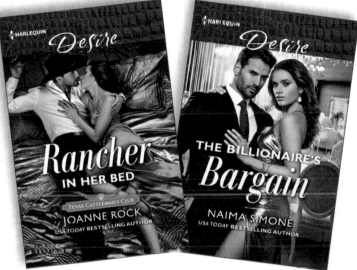

Get 2 FREE Books

See inside for details.

Dear Reader,

Since you are a lover of our books, your opinions are important to us... and so is your time.

That's why we made sure your **"FAST FIVE" READER SURVEY** can be completed in just a few minutes. Your answers to the five questions will help us remain at the forefront of women's fiction.

And, as a thank-you for participating, we'd like to send you **4 FREE THANK-YOU GIFTS!**

Enjoy your gifts with our appreciation,

Pam Powers

To get your
4 FREE THANK-YOU GIFTS:

✱ Quickly complete the "Fast Five" Reader Survey
and return the insert.

"FAST FIVE" READER SURVEY

1 Do you sometimes read a book a second or third time? ○ Yes ○ No

2 Do you often choose reading over other forms of entertainment such as television? ○ Yes ○ No

3 When you were a child, did someone regularly read aloud to you? ○ Yes ○ No

4 Do you sometimes take a book with you when you travel outside the home? ○ Yes ○ No

5 In addition to books, do you regularly read newspapers and magazines? ○ Yes ○ No

YES! I have completed the above Reader Survey. Please send me my 4 FREE GIFTS (gifts worth over $20 retail). I understand that I am under no obligation to buy anything, as explained on the back of this card.

225/326 HDL GNQC

FIRST NAME

LAST NAME

ADDRESS

APT.#

CITY

STATE/PROV.

ZIP/POSTAL CODE

▲ If offer card is missing write to: Reader Service, P.O. Box 1341, Buffalo, NY 14240-8531 or visit www.ReaderService.com ▲

BUSINESS REPLY MAIL
FIRST-CLASS MAIL   PERMIT NO. 717   BUFFALO, NY

POSTAGE WILL BE PAID BY ADDRESSEE

READER SERVICE
PO BOX 1341
BUFFALO NY 14240-8571

NO POSTAGE
NECESSARY
IF MAILED
IN THE
UNITED STATES

"That's what happens when you're wealthy. People start thinking the worst of you."

"Really?"

"Happened a lot in my family. Before Drea learned the truth, she believed my father swindled Drew out of his ranch, Thundering Hills. Yet, all my father was trying to do was protect her from the truth. Drew had gone through quite a rough patch after his wife died and he'd made a secret deal with my dad to buy his ranch and put the money away for Drea's education. Drea wasn't told the truth until she fell in love with Mason."

"It was hard on Drea when her mom died. So, when you were talking with Mason the other night at dinner about how your father welcomed competition, you were speaking the truth?"

"Yes, my father was a fair man…to an extent. He always protected the town and made sure that the townsfolk came before dollar signs. It's how Boone Springs has thrived."

"And you and your brothers follow in his footsteps?"

"We try."

"I've always felt blessed that my shop has done so well. I thought for sure another bakery would've opened up by now. We're a growing community and—"

"You don't have to worry about that, Katie."

"What?" There was something in his tone, a finality in his voice, that worried her. She nibbled on her lip.

"You're the best baker in Texas."

"I'm sure I'm not. But just then, you seemed so confident. What are you not telling me?"

"Nothing, sweetheart. Just drop it."

"Luke, there's five bakeries in Willow County and I always wondered why I'm lucky enough to have a monopoly on the bakery business in Boone Springs."

"The grocery stores sell baked goods."

"Not the same thing. I've been in business almost seven years and in all that time, no one has tried to open a bakery that I know of. I think I'll ask April why that is." April, soon to be Risk's wife, was a Realtor. She knew both Willow and Boone counties very well. "She should know."

"Maybe, or maybe you should just count your lucky stars."

"What does that mean?"

"Nothing, sweetheart. Just don't involve April in this."

"In what?" Luke was being obtuse, deliberately trying to hide something. He kept his lips buttoned up tight.

When he reached for her, she pulled away. "Tell me."

He sighed and scrubbed his jaw. "You know the Boones own more than half of the properties in town."

"Yes, common knowledge. So?"

"So, we have a plan for the town, and each one of us has input."

"Okay?"

"That's it, Katie."

Baffled, she shook her head. "What's it?" Then a thought flashed in her mind and she couldn't let it go. She had to find out the truth no matter how the notion sickened her. "Are you saying the Boones have made sure I've had no competition?"

"Not the Boones. Just me," he said on an uncharacteristic squeak.

"Just you?" She didn't understand. Luke was confusing the hell out of her. "Why on earth would you do that?"

"It's not a bad thing, Katie. We've only had two inquiries and, well, they found better deals elsewhere."

"Because you made sure of it." Katie's emotions ran rampant. Anger, disappointment, betrayal. All of it made her heart ache. She rose from bed and threw on her clothes quickly.

"Katie."

"Get dressed, Luke. Right now."

As she watched him put on his clothes, she shook uncontrollably. Now that he was dressed and she didn't have to look at his striking body, she tried to make sense of this. She stood across the bed from him. "When did you do this? And I want the absolute truth?"

"Five years ago."

"Five," she whispered. *Five.* Frustrated, tears welled in her eyes. "Why, Luke? I don't understand."

"Don't you, Katie? Don't you know?"

She shook her head. She had no clue. Five years ago, he was dating her sister. Five years ago, he'd abandoned her sister. Five years ago, he'd joined the Marines.

Luke walked around the bed and came to face her. He placed his hands on her shoulders and she was forced to look into his melt-your-heart blue eyes. "Katie, I'm in love with you."

"No!"

"I am. And I've been in love with you for a very long time."

Oh God. She was afraid to ask. "H-how long?"

"More than five years now. When I realized I loved you, I had to back out of the wedding. I had to. I knew it was crazy and impossible. And so… I left town."

"That's why you joined the service?" She trembled from head to foot.

"Yes," he said on a long breath as if he was finally relieved to confess it. He stroked her arms up and down.

And then it all dawned on her and she flipped his arms off her and backed away. She was the reason Shelly's heart had been broken. "Oh no. Oh no. Oh no." She couldn't believe this. She couldn't comprehend what he was saying. But she knew deep down in her heart it was true. It all made sense now. "I never encouraged you."

"You didn't have to, Katie. You were just you."

"God, Luke. This is making me sick. Really sick. You have no idea how hurt Shelly was, how hard those first few years were for her. And now I find out it's all because of me! I'm to blame for all her pain." Tears streamed from her eyes now, big salty drops spilling down her cheeks.

"Nobody's to blame, Katie. You can't help who you fall in love with."

"Obviously you couldn't. And I'm not forgetting your duplicity about the bakery either. My goodness…you are certainly not like your father. You don't play fair."

Luke's eyes grew hot and he clenched his teeth. "All I wanted was for you to have a good life, Katie. I wanted you to be happy, to be successful."

"And you didn't think enough of me to let me go after that success on my own."

"My God, woman. You are being irrational."

"I'm being real, Luke. And honest. I don't want you to love me. I want a divorce as quickly as possible. And I want you to leave."

Luke looked her square in the eyes. "Fine."

"Well, good. Now go."

"I'm gone," he said.

After he slammed the door behind him, Katie's stomach gripped tight and she raced to the bathroom, throwing up into the toilet until there was nothing left.

Six

Katie stared at the stick in her hand, looking at it hard and praying the results would miraculously change, but that was too much to hope for. The stick wasn't changing, nor had it changed the last two times she'd taken the pregnancy test this week. The nausea, her late period and three pregnancy tests weren't wrong. She was going to have Luke's baby.

Luke, the guy who'd proclaimed his love for her last week. Luke, the guy who'd made sure her bakery wouldn't fail, regardless of her talent. Luke, the guy who'd caused her family undue heartache.

She fought the guilt that was eating away at her. What would Shelly think? What would she say?

Katie searched her mind, struggling with her memory, trying to recall her interactions with Luke back when he and Shelly were dating. Had Katie somehow given him the wrong idea? Had she done anything to encourage him? She wasn't a flirt. She'd never been good in that department. No incidents came to mind, except her times working with him at the Red Barrel and sharing their love of horses.

It was hard to believe any of this, but now reality was staring her in the face on that stick.

Trembling, she touched a hand to her belly. Where could she turn? Who could she confide in? Drea was going to be married into the Boone family in a few weeks. Katie couldn't tell her best friend, could she? She certainly couldn't tell her sister or her mother, that was for sure. The news could very well send her mama back into the hospital.

"Oh, Katie, what are you going to do now? You're pregnant." Saying those words out loud, no matter how quietly, had impact. It made it real and there was no going back, no way to fix this.

She stared at herself in the bathroom mirror. How much longer could she hide her fatigue and nausea? And soon, she'd have a baby bump to hide as well. She had always wanted children, she wanted this one. It wasn't the baby's fault she'd gotten into this complicated mess. The child would be loved. Always loved.

A knock on her door made her jump. She tossed the box into the trash and straightened up her appearance.

"It's me, Drea," her friend called out.

Katie squeezed her eyes closed. Was it that time already? She was supposed to be dressed and ready to go with Drea for the final fitting on her wedding gown, but she was moving slowly this afternoon. "Coming," she said.

She opened the door and Drea took in her appearance. Oversize sweats weren't what she usually wore to go out. And well, Katie's face probably blended in with the shabby chic color on her walls. Only the paint was in style, and Katie was anything but.

Drea's big smile faded. "Katie, are you okay? You look a little...under the weather."

Of course her friend would think that. Perky Katie was always ready for anything. She worked ten hours a day and ran around town like a spark was lit under her butt. She could juggle her career and her volunteer work and still have energy to spare.

"Nope, I'm fine," she said. "Come in."

"Okay, but we don't have to rush. We don't need to be at Clara's Bridal for an hour."

That sounded good to her. She still needed to get dressed and rushing around wasn't in the plan. "I've made a pot of jasmine tea. Would you like some?"

"Yes, sounds wonderful."

"Want anything to go with it?"

"No cupcakes for me. Remember, I have to get into my wedding gown today." Drea made herself comfortable at the kitchen table and Katie brought over her rose-patterned teapot. She sat down, too and poured the tea. "You have such a sweet expression on your face right now. I think love has gone to your head."

"I have to keep pinching myself that I'm getting such a great guy. Say, when we're through at Clara's, would you like to have dinner at the ranch with all of us?"

It was the last thing she wanted to do. She hadn't seen Luke in a week, and she'd rather it stay that way. After their last encounter, she'd contacted an attorney about the divorce, but that was just in the early stages. At least she was doing something about it. "Uh, I don't think so, but thanks anyway."

Drea pierced her with a curious look. "You look about as glum as Luke does. What's with the sour puss, my friend? Is something going on between the two of you? Because if it is, I'm here to listen."

Luke was in a bad mood lately? Why? Because she'd tossed him out of her apartment when he'd shocked her with his declaration of love? How on earth did he expect her to absorb that news? And now her best friend was asking probing questions.

"Oh, would you look at the time? I'd better change my clothes and get ready. Don't want to be late. I'll just be a few minutes."

Katie escaped Drea's questioning stare and walked into her bedroom. Her shoulders slumped and all the energy seemed to drain from her body. What in the world was she going to do?

"One thing at a time," she whispered. And right now, she had to put on a happy face and be the best maid of honor she could possibly be.

She took some time to gather her thoughts and then put on a floral sundress. She tossed her arms through a cropped sunny yellow sweater and slipped into a pair of pumps. Next, she rimmed her lips with rosy gloss and colored her lids with eye shadow, hoping to hide her pale complexion. Then she scooped her hair up in a twisty bun and was good to go.

On a deep sigh, she walked out of the bedroom. "I'm ready," she called out and found Drea just coming out of the bathroom.

"Apparently that's not all you are," she said, sympathy touching her eyes. She lifted the empty pregnancy test box. "I wasn't snooping, honest. But I saw this in your trash can, honey. Are you?"

Katie squeezed her eyes closed. She hadn't wanted to tell anyone, not yet. But now she was trapped and maybe that wasn't such a bad thing. She needed a friend, someone to confide in. "I am. I mean, I think so. Three pregnancy tests wouldn't lie, would they?"

"Do you have other symptoms?"

Katie nodded.

Drea walked over to her and gave her a big hug. "Oh, Katie." The embrace lasted a long time and then Drea broke away. "Can you tell me about it?"

"We have to go to your fitting. It's important."

"You're more important. I'll change the appointment for tomorrow, not to worry." She pulled out her phone and called the bridal shop. They seemed to be accommodating her, and Katie felt terrible letting her friend down this way.

After she ended the call, Drea took her by the hand. "Now, come sit down on the sofa and talk to me." They sat facing each other. "I have a feeling Luke is the father. Am I right?"

"Yes, you're right," Katie said. "It's a long story."

"I'm here to listen. You can trust me."

"Luke doesn't know. And he can't know. Not until I can divorce him."

Drea blinked several times, shock stealing over her face. "Divorce him? Katie, you married Luke?"

She nodded, her emotions a wreck. Tears built up behind her eyes. "It's not what you think. It's worse. And I have to swear you to secrecy, Drea. Nobody else can know right now."

"Not even Mason?"

Several tears spilled down her cheeks. "You see, that's why I couldn't tell you. I don't want to put you in a compromising position. You shouldn't have to keep secrets from your fiancé."

"I, uh, I promise I won't say anything…until you tell me I can. Right now, you need my help and I need to be here for you." Drea took her hands and gave a gentle squeeze. "I want to help."

Katie nodded. "T-thank you. I know this isn't e-easy for you."

"I'm going to be fine, it's you I'm worried about. Now start from the beginning and tell me everything."

Katie started talking, the words spilling out of her mouth easily now that she was finally able to unburden herself and share her innermost secrets with her best friend.

Luke sat as his desk at Boone Inc. staring at the computer screen, too absorbed in what he was about to do to concentrate on work. He glanced at his watch. It was almost time for him to end his marriage to Katie. However short-lived, he'd loved thinking of her as his wife. But that would be over soon. His attorney was due any second now.

Luke rose from his desk and walked over to the stocked bar in the corner of his office. He picked out the finest bourbon on the shelf and poured himself a drink. He needed fortification today to go through with this. It was what Katie wanted and the last thing she'd said to him as he'd walked out her door. She didn't want his love. She wanted a divorce.

And now he was about to grant her wish.

He took a large gulp. The alcohol burned this throat going down, but it also helped soothe his wrecked heart. He couldn't hold on to Katie if she didn't want him. Didn't love him.

Only, he believed she did. She was just too frightened to admit it.

Katie wasn't easy. She wouldn't have made love to him if she wasn't emotionally involved. He knew by the way she sizzled from his touch, the way she'd kissed him back so passionately she'd nearly bowled him over. The way she'd granted him her body so generously when he'd worshipped her. It wasn't just sex between them but if she refused to admit her feelings, what else could he do?

Every bone in his body rebelled at what was about to happen, but he cared about her enough to let her go. To free her from their secret marriage so she wouldn't lose the love of her sister, her mother.

The knock on the door came too quickly. He swallowed another swig of his drink. "Come in," he said, setting the tumbler down on his desk. He stared at the door as if it'd bite him and was relieved to find his brother Risk walking in instead of Carmine Valencia, his attorney.

"Hey," Risk said.

"Hey back at ya. What's up?"

"Nothing much. April's out with the rest of the bridesmaids, going for fittings or something. Want to have lunch at the Farmhouse Grill? My treat. I have a few hours to kill and I'm craving their pulled pork sliders."

Luke shook his head. He'd deliberately set his appointment with Carmine in the Boone Inc. offices rather than at Rising Springs. It wouldn't do to parade his lawyer in front of his relatives. "Sorry, no can do. I have an appointment in a little while."

"Someone more important than your brother?" Risk chuckled and then glanced at the near empty bourbon tumbler on his desk. "You're drinking this early? Whenever I used to drink before four, it had something to do with a woman."

"Those days are over for you. Lucky you."

Risk moved farther into the room and pinned him with a sober look. "Hey, why the bitterness? What's going on?"

Luke sighed. "Nothin'."

"Something. Who is she?"

"Mind your beeswax, Risker."

"Using my childhood name that always got on my nerves? Okay, now I know there's something wrong."

"Listen, Carmine will be here any second. So, I can't have lunch with you. Sorry, bro."

"Carmine, as in your personal attorney?"

"Yep."

"Are you okay? You've been quiet and, well, grumpy this past week or so."

Luke put on a smile. "I'm fine. Just let it be, Risk. Will you?"

His brother eyed him, concern in his expression. It was hard to fool his brothers. "Yeah, but…"

"I know. If I need your help, I'll ask. But trust me, this isn't anything you can fix."

Nobody could.

Luke's mood was about to go from gray to black. As soon as Valencia walked into the office and started the divorce proceedings.

Two days later, Luke drove to Red Barrel Rescue. In many ways the rescue had rescued him, giving him an outlet for his loneliness. Giving him a chance to think without anyone asking questions or judging him. Helping heal the neglected and sickly horses put life in perspective. It gave him balance and helped him recover from the hard times he'd had in Afghanistan, the soldiers who'd been left behind. While he was in the Marines, he'd longed for home, for Katie, and the hardest part of it all was not being able to tell another soul what he was going through. He'd kept his secret love for her locked away.

And now after making arrangements with his attorney, the divorce was in motion.

Even though Katie didn't want anything from him, he'd made a few stipulations that he believed to be fair. He wasn't going to leave Katie in the lurch. If she wanted a divorce, she'd have to agree to his terms.

Luke parked his truck and waved at Wes, who was in one of the corrals trying to calm a horse. The horse snorted and paced back and forth, a frightened look in her eyes. Wes wasn't making too much progress with her.

Luke walked over to the fence and Wes approached. "Hello, Luke."

He gave Wes a nod. "Looks like you've got a new guest."

"We do. She's a feisty one. Mustang. Probably lost her way coming down from the hills. Either that or someone figured she was too wild to deal with and left her stranded. She was brought in two days ago."

"Does she have a name?"

He laughed. "Katie stopped by yesterday for a bit. She named her Cinnamon."

Luke smiled as he watched the mare huff and stomp around the far side of the corral. "That sounds about right."

"Katie tried to work with her a bit, but it was no use. The mare wouldn't let her get close. I don't know which of the two females was more stubborn. Anyway, Katie didn't look so good, so I sent her home."

Luke swiveled his head toward Wes. "How so?"

"She looked worn out, sort of drained. Never seen her look that way before. That girl does too much."

"She loves coming here." Luke always liked watching her work with the animals, whether it was to exercise them around the corrals, or bathe and groom them, or give them the loving caresses they needed. He enjoyed working beside her, seeing her energy and compassion. But it worried him a bit that she was fatigued. He wondered if she'd feel better once she received his divorce papers. It hurt to think it, but being rid of him might just be good for her health.

"We love having her here. Hell, she once told me this place was like her second home."

"I believe that." He sighed. He hadn't laid eyes on Katie in nine days and he missed her like crazy. "Well, I'm here and have a few hours. Put me to work."

Wes gave it some thought. "Pepper's up next. She could stand to take a dozen turns around the corral with the lead rope. After that, all the horses are due for their feed."

"You got it. No mucking for me today?"

"You feel like mucking?"

"Nobody feels like mucking." Except he wouldn't mind yielding a hoe and working up a sweat in the stables. Anything to take his mind off Katie.

After several hours of hard work at Red Barrel, Luke arrived home after eight and headed straight for the shower. He'd mucked after all, needing the hard work, needing to blow off steam, and now his whole body ached. He walked into the shower and lingered, the hot spray raining down his shoulders and chest.

But every time he closed his eyes, he saw Katie. He wanted her here, with him now, giving both their bodies a good washing and afterward…

Luke shook his head, trying to clear his mind of her. He had to get a grip.

The shower door latched behind him as he got out and dried off. He put on his jeans and a T-shirt and wandered downstairs. The house was unusually quiet for this time of night. No lights were on anywhere, which was how he liked it. Quiet and dark, like his mood. His stomach growled. He hadn't eaten lunch or dinner today and he needed sustenance.

As he headed toward the kitchen, he heard Drea conversing with someone and stopped just short of the doorway, not wanting to interrupt.

"I'm sneaking a bite of lemon chiffon pie," he heard her say quietly.

He realized Drea was speaking on the phone. He turned around to leave, and then Drea said, "Whoops. Sorry, Katie. I shouldn't mention food when you're nauseous. I heard the nausea and fatigue will pass after your first trimester. It's still so hard for me to wrap my head around. You're going to have a baby."

Luke's eyes opened wide. He slumped silently against the wall, shocked at what he was hearing.

"No, I promised you, I won't tell a soul," Drea whispered so quietly he could barely hear. "Not until you're ready."

Luke backed away from the kitchen doorway, his mind racing. Katie was pregnant? She was going to have his baby. Climbing the stairs, he tried not to make a sound. Once he reached his bedroom, he lowered himself down on the bed. After the shock wore off, pure joy filled him up.

It was what he'd dreamed about for so many nights.

To have a family with Katie. To *be* a family. Luke closed his eyes, absorbing the news.

But his joy only lasted an instant. Why hadn't she told him? How long had she known? She'd pressed for a divorce over and over again. Did she hate him that much to deny him their baby? Or was it fear that kept her from revealing the truth to him?

No wonder Katie had been tired lately. No wonder she'd been emotional. He'd seen a subtle change in her lately, but he'd always thought it was their secret marriage causing her stress. Well, stress or no stress, Luke wasn't giving her a divorce. Not now. Not when there was a baby to consider.

His baby. His child. A Boone.

Thoughts ran rampant in his head. Should he confront her? Make her fess up? Prod her into a confession?

He was no bully. He wanted Katie to tell him on her own. He wanted to be a part of the pregnancy, a part of the birth of his child. Did he have it in him to wait it out? Hell, he didn't know. He needed advice and he needed it quick. There was only one person who would know what to do.

Aunt Lottie.

The next morning, Luke put on his walking shoes and caught Aunt Lottie just as she was about to take her morning walk. "Mind if I join you today?"

His aunt tried to hide her surprise. "Sure, I'd love that." She eyed him curiously but with a smile on her face.

"Thanks."

"I remember a time when you three young boys would hike way up to the ridge with me. I loved taking you for walks."

"And you'd turn your head and pretend not to see us all roll down the grassy hill and crash into each other." The image made him smile. "It's a good memory."

"It is."

He opened the door for her and they made their way down the road. His aunt was always stylish no matter what she was doing. Today, she wore a dark raspberry jogging suit, her blond hair pulled back in a perky ponytail, her shoes sparkling clean as if she'd never worn them a day in her life, while he knew better.

"It's hard to believe Mason is getting married in a week," she said. "I know your folks will be dancing at their wedding."

"They will, if Mom has anything to say about it."

Aunt Lottie looked off in the distance. "I miss them."

"Me, too."

They were quiet for a while, and then when they were far away from the house, and out of earshot of the crew, Aunt Lottie spoke up. "As much as I love having your company on this walk, I know something's troubling you, Luke. Care to share it with me?"

"Aunt Lottie, you're sure perceptive."

"I just know you boys. And unless I miss my guess, this has something to do with that adorable girl, Katie."

Luke drew breath in his lungs. "It does. I married her."

"You married her?" His aunt stopped walking and tried her best poker face, but the shock in her voice gave her away.

"When we were in Vegas. It's the cliché drunken-vows-at-the-Midnight-Chapel sort of deal. Nobody knows. Well, one other person knows, but I'm in terrible need of advice."

Aunt Lottie nodded her head. "Why do I think you're not too sorry about this marriage?"

"Because I'm not. I'm in love with Katie."

"Oh dear," she said. "I see the problem. Katie's family won't abide that."

"They have no love for me, as you know. But actually, that's not the problem. The real problem is that I just found out by total accident, that…that Katie is pregnant."

"Pregnant? Oh my." Aunt Lottie smiled. "It's a blessing, Luke. Babies are little miracles. But does that mean she hasn't told you?"

"Right, she hasn't told me. I just found out last night by overhearing a conversation. And well, Katie's been pressing me for a divorce. She's worried about her family's reaction and what the news of our secret marriage would do to her mother's health.

"Honestly, Aunt Lottie, I think Katie is running scared. I know there are strong feelings there. She's just afraid to admit it. Now I don't know what to do. I've spoken to my attorney about filing for a divorce, putting the wheels in motion because Katie wanted to have this whole thing behind her. Unfortunately, my attorney is too efficient, and the papers have already been sent. But I won't sign them. I won't divorce her now that she's carrying my child. But do I confront her about the baby?"

"Oh dear. Luke, I understand your impatience. But Katie is in a tough spot right now. She's probably as confused as you are. Don't put more pressure on her. Give her time to sort it out in her head. She'll do the right thing."

He ran a hand through his hair and sighed. "That's easier said than done."

"I know." She turned to him, wrapping her arms around his shoulders, lending support and love. "Be patient with her. In the end, she'll be grateful for it. And one more thing."

"What is it?"

"Don't you dare divorce that girl."

He laughed, feeling a lightheartedness he hadn't felt in a long while. "I don't plan to."

Katie fumed, staring at the divorce papers she'd received by special messenger today. She couldn't believe the terms Luke expected her to agree to. What was with that man, anyway? Their marriage wasn't real. It had been a big fat mistake. She'd told him she wanted nothing from him, not one thing. But did Luke listen? No. He'd had his attorney draw up papers that went totally against her wishes.

She wouldn't agree to his crazy terms. She picked up her phone and tapped out a text to him.

I need to see you, right away.

Her text was answered five minutes later. I can be there in half an hour.

She didn't want Luke coming up to her apartment. She'd been getting curious looks from Lori lately, but her friend and employee was too discreet to question her. Aside from that, Katie didn't want reminders of the last time they'd been together in her apartment.

She didn't love the idea of meeting him in a restaurant either. There were too many people who might overhear their conversation. She couldn't believe she'd had to resort to so much secrecy lately.

Not here, she texted. Meet me at Red Barrel in an hour.

Luke's text came in fast. I'll be there.

A short time later, Katie's anger still simmered just under the surface as she drove up to the rescue. She parked her car next to Luke's steel gray truck in the back of the parking lot. Apparently, he'd gotten here early and as she scanned the area, she found him leaning against the barn wall, the sight of him making her heart beat harder. Angry or not, whenever she spotted him, her initial reaction was breathless attraction, one she couldn't quite seem to shake. It ticked her off that her body betrayed her mind.

She hadn't seen him in over a week, but now his eyes held hers from across the yard, watching her every move. She grabbed her skinny briefcase out of the car, one that made her look professional. Luke pulled away from the wall, his tan hat low on his forehead, his swagger making her swallow down hard. Dressed in jeans, a tan chambray shirt and snakeskin boots, he epitomized Texas, the image of a man who knew strength and power.

He approached her, his intense sky blue eyes trained on her. She held firm, trying not to let her heart overrule her mission here.

"Katie, it's good to see you."

She swallowed. "Hello, Luke."

"You want to talk?"

"Yes, I do."

"There's no one in the barn right now."

Privacy was of the utmost importance to her and the barn would provide that. It was a slow time for the rescue. Most of the volunteers had already gone home. And Wes was usually in the office by now, finishing up on business.

"Let's go," she said.

"How are you feeling?" Luke asked as they headed for the barn.

"Me? I'm fine."

"It's just that you've been feeling tired lately."

"No more than usual," she fibbed.

Luke nodded and was quiet until they entered the barn. Once inside she stopped, shaking her head at his gesture for them to sit on a bale of hay.

He frowned and faced her.

She pulled out the divorce papers and held them tight in her hands. "This is not what we agreed on."

"What's wrong?"

"What's wrong is that you are proposing to give me half a million dollars and then pay monthly alimony of three thousand dollars! I can't take that. I told you I wanted nothing and I meant it. I do fine on my own. At least I thought the bakery was doing well until I found out why."

"You'd be successful regardless. Can't you forget about that?"

"No, I can't. I feel terribly betrayed. I feel like a fraud, like my hard work didn't mean anything, I was pretty much ensured a monopoly in Boone Springs. The idea keeps me up at night."

"Katie, dammit. You need to rest."

Her jaw dropped. Was he kidding? He was responsible for many of her sleepless nights. "Then stop making me crazy. I don't need your help or your money."

His mouth grew tight for a few seconds, his face tensing up. And then all of a sudden, his eyes softened, the dark blue hue turning lighter, brighter. A big smile graced his face. "You know something, you're totally right, sweetheart." He took the divorce papers out of her hand. "This is all wrong."

He tore the paper down the center, then neatly placed the two pieces together and tore them again. "Here you go," he said, giving the squares back to her.

She stared at the ripped papers in her hand. "What are you doing?"

"I'm trying to give you what you want."

"No... I don't think that's it. You gave in too easily. What are you up to?"

"Nothing at all. You didn't want what I was offering. We have no deal now."

"For heaven's sake, Luke. It's not a deal, it's a divorce."

"One in the same."

A grotesque shrieking sound coming from outside interrupted them. It was so loud and ungodly, she had to find out what it was. She ran to the barn door and looked outside to the corral.

A giant hawk was swooping down on Cinnamon, winging over the horse inches from her head. The mare backed up and huffed, whinnying in panic as the bird continued to terrorize her. The hawk didn't back down. It kept on swooping and screeching at the horse.

Katie raced to the fence and screamed at the hawk. "Go! Get out of here!" She called to Luke, "He's relentless!"

Luke ran past her and the next thing she knew, he was behind the butt end of a rifle, taking aim.

"You're not going to shoot him, are you?"

He took his shot, the sharp snap of gunfire exploding in her ears. The hawk flew away, leaving the mare in peace finally.

"You didn't miss, did you?"

"Nope, wasn't trying to kill it. Just scare the damn thing away."

"I've never seen anything like that. Have you?"

"It's nothing more than a mama protecting her young, I'd imagine. There must be a nest around here. Or maybe one of her young'uns fell from the nest and Mama took it out on the closest one around."

"Cinnamon?"

"Just speculating."

She pointed at the rifle Luke held in one hand. "Where did you get that?"

"From my truck. I didn't see Wes's car and figured he was gone. It was up to me to take care of it."

"Well, that you did." She swallowed. "Could you please put it away?"

Surprise registered on his face. "Sure thing. I'll be a minute."

He turned and walked off, and Katie took a good look at the mare. She was still, motionless as if the hawk had put her in a state of shock. Maybe it was the loud ring of the rifle as well.

Katie opened the corral fence, looking into the mare's eyes. She didn't flinch, didn't seem to mind her approach. "Easy, girl, I'm coming," she said. She took several more steps toward Cinnamon. "That's it. Good girl."

She was making progress, speaking to the mare as she inched closer and closer.

"Katie, get out of there. Now." Luke's voice came from behind.

"Be quiet. She's letting me approach."

"You don't need to approach her. She's a wild one," he said through gritted teeth. Katie didn't dare turn to look at him. He was following her around the corral fencing.

"Not now, she's not. Stay put, Luke."

"Like hell I will."

"She'll spook if you try to come in and you know it."

"Are you *trying* to give me a damn heart attack?"

She smiled. He was being melodramatic. Katie knew horses just as well as anyone in Boone Springs, and she knew this one was ready to make friends.

"There, there, girl," she said softly. She put out her hand. "We're gonna be friends, you and me."

The horse snorted.

Katie waited and finally Cinnamon took a step toward her and then another step. The horse kept her eyes trained on her. Katie did the same. They were forming a bond, trusting each other, although tentatively.

Finally, the horse halted, going as far as she trusted, and Katie took the final step toward her. Inching closer, she touched her palm to the mare's nose. The mare held still as Katie stroked her up and down. "You're a good girl, aren't you?"

"Katie, you proved your point. Now get out of there." Luke's voice was low and strained.

"I know what I'm doing," she murmured.

Just then a blue jay flitted over Cinnamon's head. After what she'd just been through with the hawk, the horse spooked and kicked up her front legs. She came down hard and slammed into Katie's side. The jolt tossed her onto the packed ground. "Ow!"

"Dammit." Luke catapulted over the fence and scooped her up. "You are insane," he said, as he carried her out of the corral. He latched the gate, gave one deadly look over his shoulder at Cinnamon and headed to the barn.

The sun was setting now, casting long shadows on the land. Whatever sunshine was left didn't follow them into the barn. Katie could only make out the lines of fury around Luke's mouth, the dangerous slant of his eyes.

"You can put me down now," she said quietly.

"Can I?" His voice was harsh, impatient. "Maybe you'll decide to do another fool thing, like chase after a mountain lion or wrestle a bear."

"Luke."

"Hell. Are you hurt?" He kept her close and let her

down slowly, her body brushing against his. Once her boots hit the ground, he probed her shoulders, her arms, gently applying pressure to her rib area. "Any pain here?" he asked.

"No."

Reaching behind her, he checked her spine and lower back, then laid his hands on her buttocks. "Here?"

She cleared her throat. "Nothing hurts."

Yet his touch was familiar, comforting and welcome. She couldn't lie to herself anymore. Her body came alive under his touch.

"Thank God for that. You could've been crushed."

"But I wasn't."

"Pure luck." His anger mingled with a look of genuine relief. "Don't worry me like that again."

Katie absorbed his words. She should be spitting mad at him for making demands he had no right making, yet she wasn't mad at all. His concern touched her deeply. She couldn't remember feeling this way about anyone before or having someone care so much for her. She approached him and laid her head on his chest, enjoying the sweet sensations rushing through her. She'd never admit it to him, but when the mare bucked up and then came down, Katie froze, knowing she was going to get shoved. And she'd sent up prayers that the jolt wouldn't harm the baby she carried.

She'd been lucky her prayers were answered.

Luke stroked her back, letting his hands glide up and down, easing the rough knock she'd taken. It felt right all of a sudden, more right than it should, and she gave in to the comfort.

He tipped her chin up and claimed her mouth in an inspiring kiss. He tasted delicious and her yearnings heightened, her breaths came faster. Luke broke off the kiss and grabbed her hand. "Come with me," he said.

He tugged her to the back of the barn and grabbed a quilted horse blanket. Throwing it down over a bed of straw, he straightened it out a bit, then lay down, bringing her with him.

She turned to him. "What about Wes?"

"He's gone. I told him earlier I'd lock up for him if he had to leave. We're alone here."

They weren't entirely alone. An image flashed in her mind of the three of them becoming a family, her, Luke and their baby. Tears burned behind her eyes. She wanted to tell him so badly about his child, about him becoming a father. But she held back. Call her a coward, but she wasn't ready for the backlash. She wasn't ready to own up to the truth. He'd expect something from her, something she couldn't really give.

She was silent for a few seconds and then Luke asked, "Sweetheart, you sure you're not hurt?"

She took his face in her hands and pressed a kiss to his lips. "No, I'm not hurt, Luke."

Then she unfastened his shirt, one snap at a time, eager to touch his skin, kiss his powerful chest. And fall deep into oblivion until the stars faded in the night sky.

Luke shed his clothes quickly, with Katie not far behind. Then he covered his body over hers, warming her up, kissing her senseless. He loved this woman and had wanted to die a thousand deaths when he saw that wild mare nearly stomp the life out of her. Katie had been lucky and he hoped to heaven she'd take better precautions next time. If not for her, for their baby.

Surely, she wouldn't do anything to endanger their child, but for a moment there, back in the corral, Luke hadn't been sure. He'd nearly blurted out that he knew about the baby, and only stark fear from seeing that mare knock Katie to the ground had shut him up.

He wanted her to come to him with the truth on her own. He didn't want to bully it out of her. Aunt Lottie had told him to be patient, and he was trying. Really trying.

Her little moans brought him back to the moment and he kissed her again, weaving his hands in her long silky blond hair. She was sweet and gentle and beautiful everywhere. He treasured every morsel of her body, caressing her breasts, their undeniable softness arousing the hell out of him. Next, he lay his palm on her belly and sweeping joy entered his heart, thinking of the child they'd both created. But he didn't linger there. He moved his hand past her navel to stroke her inner folds. She was soft there, too, and her heat caused his breath to speed up and his body to grow painfully hard.

"Katie," he murmured, finding her sweet spot. He caressed her there, over and over, her body moving wildly until she whimpered and cried out his name. There was no better sound. Then he sheathed himself and rose over her, joining their bodies.

"Ah, Katie. You feel so good."

Minutes later, he found his release, and the joy and peace that went along with it.

Katie had to be his.

There was no other way.

Seven

Katie woke with a blissful humming in her heart. The first image that came to mind was being with Luke last night. Having him inside her, and how he'd thrilled her with his masterful thrusts until they both came apart.

She sighed deeply. Then her alarm chimed, giving her notice it was time to rise and shine. Well, she didn't know about the shine part, but she rose from her bed. Luke had warned her last night she'd be sore today from the fall she took and he'd been right. Her shoulders and arms ached, but nothing hurt more than her rear end.

She readied a bath, throwing in a bath bomb scented with lavender. When she'd undressed and was just about to put her toes in to check the water, her phone pinged.

It was a text from Luke.

How are you feeling this morning? Are you sore?

Yes, a little bit. I'll live. Why are you up at this hour?

It was just after four. Luckily, so far she wasn't nauseous, but the day was young.

Thinking of you. I can come by and rub the soreness away.

Katie smiled. Wouldn't you just love that.

So much.

Sorry, have to go. Just getting in the tub.

Want company?

No thanks. Go back to sleep.

I'll dream of you. In the tub.

Katie signed off and set the phone down, the sweet humming in her heart speeding up. Last night, Luke had charmed her and she wasn't sure it was deliberate on his part, but rather an organic charm, like the way his blue eyes often set on her, as if he treasured her. She also felt it in the way he protected and cared for her.

Yet, he'd gone against her wishes for a simple divorce. She'd said she wanted nothing from him. And she didn't. She'd have to fight him on that. She wouldn't take a dime of Boone money. When they divorced, it should be as if they'd never married. A clean slate. She'd never be his wife in the real sense.

Yet, he was relentless in his pursuit, making her forget all the valid reasons she had to push him away. Her sister, her mother's health, the bakery deception.

After last night, they hadn't spoken of divorce again. Luke had simply walked her back to her car and given her a quick kiss on the lips, making her promise to get to sleep as soon as possible. He'd followed her home, just to make sure she'd arrived safely.

Of all the men in the world, why did it have to be Luke?

She stepped into the tub and slid down, luxuriating in the sweetly scented water, letting the heat soak away her soreness.

She thought about the baby she carried, just a tiny speck of life that would change her whole world. And she also thought about her carelessness in the corral. She couldn't afford another mistake like that and she was grateful Luke had been there. Grateful nothing worse had happened. She'd never take a chance like that again.

Hours later, Katie stood behind the bakery case and greeted one of her first customers of the day. "Hello again," she said.

"Hi, Katie. Remember me? Davis Moore."

Katie sure did remember him. He'd come into the bakery with Shelly one day. "I do, Dr. Moore."

"Call me Davis."

"All right. What can I do for you today?"

"I'm here for a dozen of your best cupcakes. Give me a variety of them, please."

"Okay, sure. That's easy enough."

"And throw in a few of Shelly's favorites. I think she said lemon raspberry."

"Yes, that's right. She loves them."

"Well, good."

She studied the good doctor. He was tall and nice looking and seemed pleasant enough. "So how is Boone Springs treating you so far?" she asked.

"I like it just fine. The people are friendly. And the work is satisfying."

"I'm glad to hear that."

She packed up the box and he paid for the cupcakes. And then he stood there, hesitating.

"Is there anything else I can get you?" she asked.

"Uh, well." He glanced around the shop. Other than a few customers sitting at the café tables, it was just the two of them. "Shelly's been so kind to me, making me feel welcome and all, I want to do something nice for her. Do you know her favorite flowers?"

"Not roses," she blurted. Shelly had had a fascination with roses and they'd ordered hundreds of snowy white roses for her wedding to Luke. Ever since then, she abhorred every kind of rose. "But I know she likes lilies."

"Lilies. Okay. Thanks for the tip. I might've blundered with the roses otherwise."

"I'm sure she'll appreciate the thought."

"Thanks."

"Hey, Davis?" She stopped him as he was scooping up the box, about to leave. "I just want to tell you

Shelly really admires you. The flowers will make her happy."

A big smile graced his face, and his eyes were twinkling. "Good to know."

Well, wasn't that interesting? Katie didn't mind nudging the good doctor in Shelly's direction. She hadn't told Davis Moore anything that wasn't true and if only her stubborn sister would open herself up to let someone in, Shelly might find some happiness one day.

Three days later, Katie sat in her mother's kitchen trying to disguise her queasiness. "Mama, you didn't have to cook for us." Her stomach turned just at the smell of the spaghetti and meatballs. She wasn't eating heavy meals lately, but she couldn't talk her mother out of it. It was Katie's favorite dish and her mom worked so hard at preparing it.

"I want to cook for my daughters for a change. You girls are always cooking for me. You're on your feet all day long. And goodness, Katie, you've been looking tired lately."

"I've noticed it, too," Shelly said, putting out pasta bowls. "You're looking pale. Not getting enough sleep? Or are you doing too much for Drea's wedding? There's always something happening. Can't miss it in the headlines. Whenever a Boone sneezes, the local papers feel the need to report it. They're holding the rehearsal dinner at The Baron."

"Yes, that's on Friday night."

"Soon it will be all over," Shelly said, "and you won't

have any reason to deal with Luke. It must be so awkward for you."

"It…is. But we've—"

"You've what?" her mother asked, sitting up straighter in her chair. Her mother appeared healthier today, which also meant she was more engaged in the conversation.

"We've, uh, found a way to deal with each other. He's…not a bad person, Mama."

"Says who? Any man who breaks my daughter's heart isn't getting nominated for sainthood, I can assure you. We all embraced him and he turned his back on us."

"Mama, he didn't turn his back on you," Shelly said. "He turned away from me. He didn't love me enough."

Katie's chest tightened. She felt guiltier than ever, because she'd been actually entertaining thoughts of a life with Luke. But once again, her family brought her back to reality. If they ever found out the true reason Luke left Shelly—because he was in love with her—and that she was now carrying his child, all hell would break loose.

Funny, when she was around all this negativity, her situation looked grim, but when she was with Luke, she could envision a happy life together.

It was all so very confusing.

"That man doesn't know what he's lost," her mother said.

"I don't think he cares," Shelly said.

"He cares," Katie blurted.

Both heads turned to her. "What?" her sister asked.

"I mean, Luke isn't a horrible person. He knows he hurt you, hurt us all, and he's sorry about it."

"And you know this how?"

"I've spent time with him, remember? At the rescue and in preparing for Drea's wedding. But he didn't want to… Oh, never mind."

Katie could tell by their narrow-eyed expressions they weren't buying any of this. And they were looking at her like she was being a traitor to the Hate Lucas Boone Club.

"You're right. There's no need to spend another second speaking of him," her mother said.

Katie wanted to skulk in the corner but she wouldn't because she was too darn curious about Davis Moore. She took a pasta plate to the stove and dished up a generous amount for her mother. "Here you go, Mama. The least I can do is serve you."

"Thank you, sweetie." Her mom smiled and it brightened her face. Katie remembered a time when her mom smiled a lot. That was a long time ago.

Once they were all sitting and Katie was pushing her pasta around the plate, she casually mentioned Shelly's new friend. "Davis Moore came into the shop the other day, Shel. Seems he does have quite a sweet tooth."

Shelly stopped eating, the fork halfway to her mouth. "I suppose he does."

"Did you get the lemon raspberry cupcakes he bought specifically for you?"

"Yes, I did."

"He seems like a nice guy. He's settling into Boone Springs well, or so he says. I guess you've been showing him around town?"

"Yes, some. He's quite remarkable, actually. Has a long list of accomplishments in—"

"He's handsome," Katie said.

"Katie, are you interested in him?" her mother asked.

Shelly squared her a look and Katie tortured her for a few seconds. "Me? No, Mama. I think you're asking the wrong daughter."

"Shelly?"

"Mama, it's nothing. I mean, I like him and he did send me a beautiful bouquet of lilies the other day as a thank-you. But we're just friends."

"I think he wants to be more than friends, Shel."

"Why, what did he say?"

"All good things," Katie answered.

Shelly blushed and her mother gave her an approving look.

It was progress, albeit very little.

But both of them still had no use for Lucas Boone and nothing Katie could say would change that.

Luke knew the exact moment Katie entered the rehearsal dinner at The Baron Hotel's Steak House because the entire dining room seemed to light up. Or maybe it was just him. Everything seemed brighter when Katie was around. She stole his breath wearing a one-shoulder black dress and tall heels, her blond hair up in a messy bun with wisps of hair framing her face.

He sighed. She still hadn't told him about the baby and his patience was coming to an end. He couldn't see any physical evidence of her pregnancy yet, but he knew their child was growing in her belly.

Didn't she know how much he'd want to be a part of it? How much he would cherish their time together until the baby came? He thought for sure they'd gotten closer after the night in the barn, but after that one text, she'd never returned any of his other calls or texts.

She was avoiding him.

Risk stood beside him as the bridesmaids entered the restaurant. They were all giggles and laughter, and right in the middle of it all was the happy bride-to-be, Drea. Soft music played in the background as the rest of the wedding party filed in.

"Guess everyone's here," Risk said. "What happens now?"

"Now we have drinks and food and Drew makes a speech."

"Isn't he doing one tomorrow?"

"Nope, that's my job," Luke said.

"I suppose Katie's giving one, too?"

"I suppose."

"Don't tell me you don't know every little thing about her, bro. She's on your radar twenty-four-seven."

"I'm in love with her, Risk. So yeah, she's on my radar. And that's just between you and me."

"Okay. Wow. Want to talk about it?"

"There's nothing to say. You know the situation with her family."

"Yeah… I do. Man, oh man. Does she feel the same way about you?"

Luke shrugged. "She's trying her best not to but yeah, I think she does."

Risk gave him a sharp slap on the back. "Hang in

there, and try not to look like you're going to your own execution. For Mason and Drea."

Luke nodded. "I'll do my best."

He wandered over to Aunt Lottie. She looked brilliant tonight in a sleek sapphire pantsuit. She always wore the most exotic jewelry from her many adventures around the globe. Today her necklace made of gold and Asian sculpted jade caught his eye. "Aunt Lottie, you're looking mighty pretty tonight."

"Thank you, Luke. That's nice to hear."

"Would you like a drink?" he asked.

"I would love one."

He guided her over to the bar. "What would you like?"

"Wine sounds wonderful. A hearty pinot," she told the bartender.

"I'll have your best rye," Luke said.

"Yes, sir."

Once the drinks were in their hands, Luke walked with Aunt Lottie over to a corner of the room. "How's your…situation, Luke?" she asked quietly, sipping her wine.

"She still hasn't told me. I have to admit, it angers me. She's denying me my rights."

"But you don't blame her, do you?"

"I'm trying not to. She's the *one*, Aunt Lottie. I can't stand just waiting around for her to come to her senses." Luke took a swig of his drink, the whiskey going down smoothly.

"Being patient isn't easy, especially when you know the truth. I'm excited for you as well. I almost can't wait

myself. You'll be the first one in the family to become…
Well, you know."

He nodded, searching the room and finding Katie
in conversation with both of his brothers. She would
talk to them but not him. A surge of jealousy had him
gulping down his drink.

"She's a pretty one, isn't she?" Aunt Lottie remarked.

"Beautiful."

His aunt touched his arm. "Be patient. It hasn't been
that long. And I'm sure Katie is mixed up right now,
trying to work things out in her head."

"I hear you," he said. "I just wish she would trust
what she feels. Trust me."

Drew walked up then, and Aunt Lottie gave him a
warm smile. "Hello, Drew. Are you ready for the big
day tomorrow?"

"I am. How about you?"

"Yes, of course. You know how I feel about Drea.
She's like the daughter I never had. I'll be very happy
seeing Mason and Drea say their vows."

"It'll be a good day. Well, I'll talk to you later. Didn't
want to interrupt your conversation."

"It's okay, Drew." Luke kissed his aunt's cheek. "You
stay and talk to Aunt Lottie. I'm about ready for another
drink. Excuse me."

Lottie watched Luke walk off, wondering if she'd
given him the right advice. She'd certainly botched her
own love life, so who was she to give him guidance
on his?

She turned to Drew. "You look nice this evening."

In his dark suit and string tie held with a sterling silver and turquoise clasp, Drew had never looked more appealing to her. His snowy hair and slight beard were groomed perfectly, giving him an air of sophistication.

"Thank you. Same goes for you," he said. "I like that color blue on you."

She smiled. "Thank you. Are you nervous about your speech?"

"I'm not much for public speaking."

"I think you'll do fine. After all, you'll be talking about Drea."

"And what a lousy father I've been."

"That's past history. Drea adores you."

"She didn't always."

"She does now and that's what you have to focus on."

"I guess so. I appreciate the pep talk. Well, just wanted to say hello. I'll be getting to my seat. Looks like dinner's about to be served."

"Sure, okay," she said, deflated. Why didn't she tell him she adored him, too? Why didn't she apologize for believing he'd been interested in another woman? The man had been nothing but true blue and honest with her, and yet she'd managed to alienate him. After the way he'd kissed her the other day, she had no doubt about his feelings for her or her feelings for him.

She just wished she had the nerve to tell him.

Before it was too late.

Katie sat next to Luke at the rehearsal dinner. There was no escaping it. Mason was paired up with Drea,

Risk with April, and she didn't want to make a big deal of changing seats.

The truth was, she was falling for Luke, and the more time she spent with him the harder it would be to say goodbye. They couldn't be a couple. They couldn't stay married.

But when the baby came, she wouldn't deny Luke his rights. Her child needed both a father and mother. She'd been deprived of that in her own childhood, and sure, she'd faired okay, but it was hardly ideal. Her child deserved better than having come from a broken home, even before he or she was born.

Unfortunately, right now it was the only way forward. After the wedding, she'd have no reason to see Luke. She'd tell him in her own way and in her own time and…she'd have to confess to her family, too. She wasn't looking forward to that. She kept praying a solution would miraculously present itself.

The impossibility of it all hit her and tears moistened her eyes.

"What's wrong, sweetheart?" Luke whispered ever so closely in her ear.

She shook her head, summoning strength. "Nothing," she whispered, making sure no one was observing their exchange. She faked a smile. "I'm fine."

And then Luke's hand found hers under the table. The comfort he lent felt good even if he was the last person who should make her feel anything. But his encouragement, his compassion, seeped into her and soothed her raw nerves. She had to think about the baby and what was best. When she was with Luke, she had trouble thinking of anything else but being with him...as a family.

And yet her worry about her mom and sister always seemed to ruin that fantasy.

Mason stood up then and thanked everyone for being a part of the wedding. He'd put gifts on the table and encouraged the groomsmen to open their small blue boxes. Luke was forced to let go of her hand to open his gift. She was hit with a wave of relief and sadness at the same time as he broke their connection.

"Gold cuff links," he said, glancing at her.

She smiled. "Those will look good on you," she said. "They're very nice." And they probably cost a fortune.

At times, she forgot about the Boone wealth and what it meant. But Luke wasn't defined by his wealth. He was down to earth and kind and generous. He ran Rising Springs Ranch, shared the corporation with his brothers and owned half the town.

He was a man's man, a guy any girl would love to have by her side.

Tears touched her eyes again. She was being hormonal, her elevator emotions going up and down.

"Hey, if you don't stop looking so sad, I might have to kiss you into a better mood," Luke said softly.

She gasped and eyed him, giving him a don't-you-dare look.

"Smile, Katie."

"For Drea and Mason?" She glanced over to where they sat at the table. They were busy eating their salads and chatting with each other, happiness on both of their faces.

He shook his head. "For me."

Goodness, what was with his ego? "I have no smiles for you," she said through tight lips.

Luke grinned. "Katie, you're forgetting about the work we did at the rescue," he said loud enough for others to hear, if they were so inclined. "You were very diligent."

Her nerves rattled. Of course, no one would know what they were talking about, but she knew, and it was a visual she couldn't get out of her head. Being naked in the barn with Luke and having him make love to her had been exciting. He'd always managed to draw her out of her wholesome shell and make her do wild and sexy things. "I…know. Sometimes I get carried away."

Luke stared into her eyes. "But it's very much appreciated."

Heat rushed to her face. "Is it?"

"Yes, you have a knack, with stallions especially, that's really inspiring."

She rolled her eyes, hiding a smile. There were no stallions at the rescue right now. "You give me too much credit."

"Doubtful."

Just then, Drea rose from her seat. "I, too, want to thank all of you for being a part of our special day. I can't wait until Mason and I become man and wife with all of you very special people in attendance. And I have gifts for my wonderful bridesmaids, too."

She walked around the room, giving the girls beautiful embossed gift bags made of soft lavender linen, the same color as their gowns. When she got to Katie, she kissed her cheek. "Thank you for everything, my bestie. This one is special, just for you. Because you're my maid of honor."

"Thank you," Katie said, giving Drea a smile straight from the heart.

"Please open your gifts," she said to everyone.

Katie opened hers by pulling a drawstring and then reached inside. She pulled out a black velvet box and opened the lid. "Ah! This is beautiful." She lifted out a gold-and-diamond drop necklace. She was touched and truly surprised. She'd never owned anything this exquisite before. "I don't know what to say."

"Say you'll wear it tomorrow."

"Try to stop me." She hugged the necklace to her chest.

Drea grinned. "I had help picking it out."

"Mason?"

She shook her head. "Luke. Actually, he has pretty good taste."

"You picked this out?" she asked him.

He nodded. "It looked like you. Bright and sparkly."

She blinked and didn't know what to say. He was constantly surprising her.

"I will treasure it," she told Drea.

An hour later, Katie walked out of the restaurant and heard footsteps hitting the ground behind her. "Katie, wait up."

She sighed, stopped and turned around to Luke. "What is it?"

"Let me walk you to your car."

"That's not necessary."

"No, but I'd like to." His jaw set tight and it was no use arguing.

"Suit yourself," she said lightly and as she began walking again he fell in step beside her. He was quiet, pensive, and she didn't know what to make of his mood.

Once she reached her Toyota in the parking lot, she spun around to face him. "Well, here I am."

"I can see that."

"Thank you for walking me. Now it's time for me to get going."

"Where to?"

"Home to pick up my things and then I'm spending the night at Drea's cottage. We're getting our hair and makeup done there in the morning. Drew's getting the place ready for us right now."

He nodded.

"I really should get going."

A tick worked in his jaw. "Katie, where do we go from here?"

There was an urgency about him that she didn't quite understand. Why was he being so persistent? "Luke." She glanced around. There were a few people getting into their cars near her. "This is hardly the time or place."

"Then you tell me a good time and place and I'll be there."

She sighed. "I don't know. We have issues. And I can't think about them at the moment. Why are you bringing this up now?"

"Because you've been avoiding me. You haven't been answering my calls or texts. I didn't want to say anything tonight, but at some point you're gonna have to face reality."

"And what reality is that?"

Luke's eyes narrowed. He opened his mouth to say something, then closed it again.

"Look, I just needed a…break," she said.

"From what?"

"From…you."

His lips went tight and the look in his eyes darkened. "From me?"

"Yes, if you must know. I can't think when you're around."

"That's right, I make you crazy."

"Yes, yes, you do and it's horrible."

His brows rose in surprise and a hurt look crossed his features. "Fine. I'll give you all the space you need," he said, his tone sullen.

"You don't have to get mad."

"I'm not mad," he said, his voice a harsh rasp. He opened her car door and gestured for her to get in. She slid into the driver's seat, giving him a last look.

Then he slammed the car door.

And refused her another glance.

Eight

Katie cried on the way to the MacDonald cottage. She wanted to shed all her tears before she spent the night with Drea. This was to be their special before-the-wedding slumber party. Just the two of them, like they'd planned since they were kids. She wouldn't spoil the fun by being a miserable companion.

But she'd hurt Luke, made him angry. And she didn't feel good about any of it: the divorce, her deception about the baby. She wasn't lying when she told Luke he made her crazy. He did, because he was the right man for her, under the wrong circumstances.

Why did it have to be him? Recently, she'd asked that of herself every single day. She couldn't take it any longer. She didn't want to hurt the people she cared about.

It was time to own up to the truth. She would reveal her secrets and finally deal with the consequences.

After the wedding.

With that thought in mind, her tears stopped flowing. At least she had a plan now and it made her feel one thousand percent better. As she entered the gates of Rising Springs Ranch, she stopped the car and tidied herself up, wiping her tears and putting on a fresh coat of lip gloss. Tonight, she would be the best, best friend to Drea she could be and they would have a fun time.

Katie started her car up again and slowly drove down the road past the main house heading to the cottage. With her maid of honor dress and shoes in the back seat as well as her toiletries, she was totally prepared.

What she wasn't prepared for was seeing the flames up ahead, blazing bright and licking the night sky.

Her throat tight, she drove farther down the road and immediately stopped when she spotted Lottie and Drea with looks of horror on their faces. She parked the car on the side of the road and ran to them, the acrid smell of soot and ash filling her lungs.

"Oh no!" Half of the cottage was on fire. "What happened?"

Drea was shaking uncontrollably. "Oh, Katie. My d-dad's in there. I don't know how it h-happened. But he left the dinner early to come home and fix up the house for us."

"Luke's gone in after him," Lottie cried out.

"Luke? Oh my God. How long has he been in there?"

"He ran in as soon as he spotted the flames. Fire-fighters are on the way, but Luke refused to wait."

Katie's heart raced. This couldn't be happening. Not to Drew and Luke. Her Luke. She'd never forgive herself if something happened to him. She should've told him…she loved him. She did. She loved him, but was too frightened to confess. And now she was scared to death she'd never get the chance to tell him.

He needed to know she was carrying his baby. She needed him to know he was going to be a father. Maybe he wouldn't have taken such a chance with his own life. But Luke was tough, a Marine, and of course he'd head straight into a burning house to save a friend.

She closed her eyes and prayed for both of them.

She couldn't lose Luke now, not when she was finally able to admit her true feelings for him.

The wind shifted and they were blasted with heat, forcing them to step back several yards. To think, Luke was in there, trying to save Drew. Smoke billowed up and they waited impatiently, holding hands, tears spilling down their cheeks.

From a distance, sirens could be heard. The fire engines were on the property now, but Katie kept her eyes trained on the front of the house. "Luke, please, please be okay," she whispered.

And then from out of the smoke and flames, Luke staggered down the steps, his face a mass of black soot, as he half walked, half dragged Drew with him.

"Thank God!" Lottie exclaimed, running over to the fence and opening it.

Both men looked worse for wear, but they were alive and breathing on their own.

"Daddy, are you okay?" Drea ran over to help.

"He will be," Luke said. "I found him knocked out on the floor by the back door. He's got a big knot on his forehead."

Drew looked up and gave his daughter half a smile. "One of the candles I set out for you gals got too close to your curtains and caught fire. I went running through the house to get the hose and tripped over a box of your softball trophies," he told her.

Drea's face paled. "Oh, Daddy. I'm so sorry."

"I wanted to surprise you and Katie with the trophies. I've been cleaning them up and damn fool that I am, I didn't quite…" He began coughing hard, his face turning red from the exertion.

"It's okay, Dad. No more talking right now."

Katie glanced at Luke. He looked exhausted, too, and coughed every now and then. She wanted to run over to him and hug him tight, but the firefighters had just pulled up and were shouting orders. Paramedics took Drew and Luke to their van for observation, while the firefighters set their hoses up to battle the flames.

Katie stood by the van, watching them tend to Luke. Every so often, he would glance her way and she'd smile and wave, wiping tears from her eyes. She'd been given a second chance with him and she wasn't going to blow it.

Lottie and Drea stood by Drew's side as he was being examined. "You really should go to the hospital for a complete checkup," the paramedic was saying.

"You said I'm fine. I don't need any more checking up."

"I said there's no sign of smoke inhalation. But that needs to be confirmed."

"My daughter is getting married tomorrow, and I need to be there."

"Dad, it won't take too long," Drea said.

"I'm just fine, Drea."

Lottie touched the paramedic's arm. "Let me speak to him, please."

"Okay, ma'am. I'll be back in a few minutes after I call this in."

Lottie smiled at Drew. "You had me in tears." She walked over to him, arms extended, and gave him a big hug. "I've never been so frightened in my life. To think you might've died in that house. And I can't have that. I can't lose you. I can't stand the thought of us not being together a moment longer. Drew Joseph MacDonald, I love you very much. And if you'll have me, I want to marry you."

Drew blinked and rubbed his sore head. "Did I hear you right? You want us to get married. Maybe I did hit my head too hard."

"Yes, yes and no. Yes, you heard me right. Yes, I want to marry you. And no, you didn't hit your head too hard. At least I hope not. You'd better say yes, because I'm not going to let you alone until you do."

"Promise?"

"I promise."

Drew smiled. It was a whopper, and Lottie smiled right back at him.

Katie and Drea exchanged glances. Drea had prayed

for her father to find happiness. Now her prayers were being answered.

"I love you, Lottie. And I'm honored to marry you," he said. "Don't know if I'll have a house for us to live in though."

"We'll figure it out. It'll be our little adventure."

"Now you've got me looking forward to having an adventure with you."

"Oh, and one more thing, Drew," Lottie said. "You need to be checked out tonight at the hospital."

"No, I don't—"

"You do. And so does Luke. But don't worry, I'll go with you and make sure you get to the wedding on time."

"Bossy woman."

"You love it."

He grinned and pulled her close. "Guess I do."

And then he kissed her.

Once the paramedics were through checking over Luke, Katie walked over to him, put her arms around his neck and kissed him solid on the mouth. She didn't care who witnessed it, or what they thought. She just wanted Luke, period.

He snuggled her close, his eyes gleaming. "Are you going to propose to me?" he asked.

She brought her mouth to his and kissed him again. "Silly man. I'm already your wife."

"But you don't want to be."

"I'm rethinking that, Luke." She smiled at him and he blinked.

"You are?"

She nodded.

Luke's expression changed and his mouth spread into a grin.

Katie put her hands on his soot-stained face, looked into his blue eyes. "You saved Drew's life. It was a brave thing to do, but it scared me half to death."

"I just reacted. I couldn't let him die inside the house. I had to go after him."

"You risked your life."

"It was worth it. And there's an added plus."

"Oh yeah? What would that be?"

"You're here with me. And your eyes have a certain gleam. Sort of like the way you'd look at Snow, or one of your delicious cupcake concoctions."

"You do realize you just compared yourself to a horse and a cupcake," she said softly, admiring his handsome face and thinking of what might have happened to him.

He chuckled. "Katie, you're too much." He bent his head and kissed her, and it was better than anything in the world. But he needed more medical attention and she needed to wrap her head around loving him. She backed away, imploring him, "Be patient with me. For just a little while longer."

Before he could respond, Drea walked up with Drew and Lottie, all three holding hands. Drea stepped up. "I'll never forget what you did tonight, Luke." She was obviously rattled, the prospect of losing her dad keeping tears in her eyes. "You're a good man."

They embraced, Drea hugging him tight.

"Does that mean I'll be your favorite brother-in-law from now on?"

Drea smiled. "Risk would have to do something pretty great to top this. Saving my dad, that's a pretty high bar."

Drew walked over to him. "Let me shake your hand, Luke." Then he swiped the air and put his hand down. "Forget that." He wound his arms around Luke and gave him a big manly hug. "Thank you, son. I wouldn't be here if it weren't for you."

"You're welcome, Drew."

"I don't know what else to say. You risked your life to save mine. I'll be grateful to you for the rest of my life."

"No need for that," Luke said humbly. "Just make Aunt Lottie happy."

"I plan to." Drew gazed at Lottie with love in his eyes. It was beautiful to witness.

Lottie gave Luke a big hug, too. "Don't know what I would've done if I lost you both. You're like a son to me and I love you very much."

"Love you, too, Aunt Lottie."

"So then you'll get checked out at the hospital?"

"I'll make sure of it," Katie intervened.

Luke grabbed her hand. "You'll go with me?"

"Yes."

And if Shelly got wind of it, she'd have to tell her the truth. But luckily, she happened to know Shelly wasn't working tonight. She was taking her mother over to her friend's house for a nice long visit. It bought Katie a little time to reveal the truth.

When Mason and Risk showed up, everyone turned

to them and filled them in on what had happened. They'd stayed behind to have drinks at The Baron before coming home.

As the fire was quelled, leaving only half of the three-bedroom cottage standing, everyone right then and there decided the wedding would go on as planned. It was set and ready to go.

They had something else to celebrate, too.

Drew and Lottie's engagement.

"I'm sorry for the way things turned out tonight, Drea." Katie handed her friend a glass of white wine. She happened to know this brand of pinot grigio was her favorite. The Boones had offered them the entire east wing of the second floor of their ranch house for tonight. They sat facing each other on the twin-size beds in one of the guest rooms. "Your dad's home is nearly destroyed."

"He'll rebuild, Katie. It'll give him and Lottie a chance to build something to their liking. Besides, I think my dad's happier than he's ever been. He and Lottie have been tiptoeing around each other for years. Now they'll finally settle down together. And he got a clean bill of health, thanks to Luke. If he hadn't rushed in to save Dad, the smoke would've gotten him before the fire did."

"Yeah, Luke's amazing. I'm happy he checked out just fine at the hospital, too. In that respect we were very lucky."

Drea smiled. "I saw you two kissing."

"I finally realized I love him. He's my guy."

"So, are you going to tell him everything?"

"I plan to. Very soon. I couldn't stand the thought of something happening to him before I had a chance to tell him he was going to be a father. It really put things in perspective for me. Our child deserves a loving home."

"I'm excited for you."

"Thanks." She bit her lip. "It's strange how things turn out sometimes, isn't it?"

"What do you mean?"

"Well, you hated Mason for what you thought he'd done to your father. And I wasn't too keen on Luke, for what he did to Shelly. Now we're both in love with a Boone."

"You married one."

"And you're about to." Katie sipped her sparkling cider. "Let's not forget how much April disliked Risk when he first came back into her life, too. Their fake engagement led to the real thing."

Drea took a sip of wine. "Well, there's just something about those Boone brothers."

"I'll drink to that." She finished off her cider. "Oh my gosh, I just realized you probably lost a lot of your things at the cottage, too."

"I did, but I have what I need. I've been staying with Mason at the house, so half my stuff is here now."

"You're not panicked so I take it your wedding dress is safe and sound."

"Lottie picked it up for me from the bridal salon. It's here, at the house. She was going to bring it by the cottage in the morning."

"Thank goodness. Tomorrow is going to be a special day."

"You know, I wouldn't mind if you decided to wander over to the west end of the floor tonight, hon. Risk is at April's tonight and Mason decided to spend the night at The Baron."

"Because the bride and groom shouldn't see each other before the wedding?"

"Right…and we like the tradition. But tradition doesn't dictate anything about the best man and the maid of honor not seeing each other."

"Really…hmm. I wouldn't want to desert you."

"I'm starting to get super tired." Drea put her arms up and yawned. "And I need my beauty sleep."

"You're such a bad liar. But I would love to check in on him. Make sure he's okay."

Drea pointed toward the door. "Go."

"Gosh, now I'm getting thrown out of your room."

"Only because you've got something much better waiting for you across the hall."

Katie stood. "How do I look?" She fussed with her hair and straightened her dress.

"You could be wearing rags and Luke would think you were beautiful. You look great." Drea shooed her away. "It's down the hall and the last door on your right."

Katie blew her a kiss and made her way down the long hallway on bare feet, eager to see Luke again.

She knocked on his bedroom door three times. No answer. He was probably sleeping. Her desire to check in on him was stronger than her worry about waking him up, so she put her hand on the doorknob and opened the door.

As she stepped inside, she told herself she had a perfect right to check on her husband. He could've been injured or killed tonight running into those flames. But as she looked around, she found his bed was still made. Had he gone somewhere at this hour of night? She turned to leave, her hand reaching for the doorknob.

"Katie, where do you think you're going?"

She froze for a second and spun around. Luke was just stepping out of the bathroom, a towel draped below his waist. Moonlight glistened on his wet hair. Drops of water cascaded down his shoulders, falling onto his granite-hard chest. She itched to touch him there, to devour him and show him how much she loved him even though she had yet to tell him. "Luke, I didn't think you were here."

"I'm here." He smiled wide.

"Y-yes, you are."

He sauntered over to her. "Some nights I like to shower in the dark, with just the moonlight streaming in. It's quiet and peaceful that way."

"Oh… I didn't know."

"There's lots of things you don't know about me, sweetheart. I can't wait for you to learn all of them." He moved closer, the scent of his lime soap wafting to her nose.

"I came to check on you."

He opened his arms wide. "I'm healthy, Katie."

Her gaze flew below his waist and the bulge hidden under the towel. "That might be an understatement, Luke."

He laughed, a mischievous sound that got her juices flowing.

"You sure you're not tired, because I don't have to stay—"

"You're joking, right?"

She smiled at him. "Y-yes, I think I am. I don't want to leave."

Luke opened his arms and she stepped into them. Someone up above was granting her wishes, because as his arms wrapped around her and snuggled her close, her every dream was coming true. There was only one tiny flaw in her plans to be with him tonight, but she shoved thoughts of her family aside. She wanted to be fully in the moment. And as Luke's lips touched hers, his hard body pressing against her and his desire under the thin towel barrier reminding her of the thrills to come, she washed away everything and everybody but what was happening between them tonight.

"Katie." His voice held awe and wonder. "This is where you're meant to be."

She overflowed with emotion. It was almost too much for her, this roller coaster of a night. She shook, unable to control herself. "Luke, just kiss me and keep on kissing me."

He gripped her head in his hands and crushed his lips over hers, his expert mouth making every bone in her body melt. She could faint from the delicious sensations he aroused. And soon her dress was off and they were on the bed, under the covers, Luke worshipping her body.

His heat was contagious. She was nearing combustion, but she held on, wanting to enjoy every minute of this night with him. A night filled only with desire. No problems, no issues, just two people expressing their love in the most potent way.

Katie's body erupted first, her orgasm reaching new heights. "Luke," she cried out.

And he was there with her, rising above, his hard body tightening up, his powerful thrusts and groans of pleasure beautiful to behold. He held her tight as his release came and she kissed him until his breaths steadied and they both fell back onto the bed.

"Wow," he said, as he ran his hand up and down her arm. "Just checking that you're real."

"I'm real. Realer than real, after that."

He laughed and kissed her shoulder. "Stay with me tonight. Be my wife in all ways."

"I will," she answered, wanting that so badly, too.

Luke looked at the empty place beside him on the bed and smiled at the note Katie had left for him this morning on her pillow.

Dear Husband,
Sorry, had to leave early. Today is all about Drea and Mason. See you soon.
Your Wife

Luke rose from the bed, breathing in Katie's pleasing scent. In his humble opinion, she always smelled delicious and today was no exception. He couldn't believe she was finally his, after all his years of trying to do right by her, of trying to deny his feelings.

She hadn't said the words he wanted to hear. She hadn't confessed her love or told him about their baby yet, but they had made great progress. Finally, Katie thought of him as her husband. She'd come to him last night, and all it had taken was him racing into a house on fire for her to realize she cared about him.

He stepped into the shower, letting the water rain down his body, wishing Katie was here. It'd been a fantasy of his, to have her all soapy and wet with him, but they had time for that. Today, his brother was getting married, and Luke had the honor of being his best man.

He dressed in jeans and a T-shirt, and glanced out the window to the yard below. A team of event workers were constructing an open-air tent to house two hundred and fifty guests. A dance floor was going up as well as tables and chairs. Mason and Drea had opted to speak their vows on the steps of the gazebo Mason had built in the backyard.

Rising Springs Ranch had hosted many events, but this was the first wedding, and the Boones were doing it big.

Luke walked down the hallway and across the bridge that led to the east wing of the house. He heard the girls giggling, Drea and Katie giddy with excitement over the wedding. Warmth spread through his heart as he made his way downstairs.

In the kitchen, Aunt Lottie was drinking coffee with Drew. Early risers. "Mornin'," he said to them. Lottie and Drew had eyes only for each other.

Then Drew sat up straighter. "Luke, boy, how are you feeling this morning?"

"I'm feeling fit. How about you?"

"I'm…doing fine. Lottie's making sure of it. She won't hear of me worrying about losing my place, not today. Much of what I lost can be replaced but today is Drea's special day. And as long as she's happy, I'm happy."

Luke gazed at the loving look on Aunt Lottie's face and knew instantly these two people were right for each other. "Congratulations again. Seems we've got another wedding coming up."

"Yep, but we're happy to focus on this one today. Drew's giving away his daughter."

"Now, Lottie, I'm not keen on that phrase. I'm not giving Drea to anyone."

Lottie laughed. "What would you call it then?"

"I'm allowing Mason the privilege of marrying my daughter."

"And Mason knows it, too," Luke added. "When's he getting here?"

"Not until just before the ceremony."

Luke poured himself a cup of coffee and looked under the covered dishes to see the brunch Jessica had made for the bridesmaids. "Wow, that's a lot of food for the girls."

"I agree, so help yourself, and then vamoose for a few hours. The girls need to get all dazzled up. Myself included."

"And men tend to ruin their party? Is that what you're saying, Aunt?"

"Something like that."

Luke got the hint. "I'll eat fast and then be on my way."

He had something he needed to do at Red Barrel Rescue anyway.

Something that would make Katie happy.

Katie stared at Drea in the oval mirror in her room, noting the gleam in her eyes, the joy on her face. All the bridesmaids had already gone downstairs, giving her and Drea some alone time.

"Drea, you are beautiful. I can't even describe how amazing you look. Now I know what they mean when they say blushing bride. That's you, and guess what? It's time to go downstairs."

"It is," she said dreamily. "I'm…a little nervous."

"No need to be. I've got your back."

"Thanks, hon." Drea gave her a peck on the cheek, making sure she didn't smudge her pale pink lipstick. "And you look amazing, too. I love your hair like that." Katie's hair was pulled up in a very loose updo, with blond curls framing her face. "The band of flowers in your hair makes you look like a princess."

"It's a miracle what a hair and makeup artist can do with a hot mess like me."

"Shush, none of that. You're not a hot mess as far as I'm concerned. You're a beautiful mommy-to-be."

Katie turned sideways and glanced at her reflection in the mirror. "Do you see a baby bump?"

Drea grinned. "Not yet, but it'll be here soon enough."

Katie sighed. She still had trouble believing she was

having a baby, and then her crazy symptoms would appear to remind her. Today, she'd been lucky: no nausea. Only bliss this morning, waking up next to Luke. She had him on the brain, but she had to remember that this day was all about Drea and Mason. "I hear the violinist playing. It's time to go."

"Okay," Drea said. "You first. I'll be right behind you."

As Katie walked out the back door and down the path leading to the gazebo, she found Mason waiting for his bride, an eager look in his eyes. Katie didn't linger on Mason but rather on the guy standing next to him, his best man, the man she'd married weeks ago. And didn't Luke look smoking hot in his tuxedo?

Katie couldn't seem to look away until the music stopped for a beat, and then the familiar wedding march began to play. Drea stood beside her father, their arms entwined. She was holding a bouquet of white gardenias and roses. Everyone stood and then Drea made the walk down the aisle.

Katie teared up, her emotions running high. This was a monumental day. Her bestie was marrying a great guy. And before she knew it, they spoke sweet, funny, loving vows to each other and were then pronounced husband and wife. It was a glorious ceremony and Katie's tears flowed freely, from happiness for a change.

Mason and Drea were met with great applause and they waved to their friends and family as they made their first walk as a married couple down the aisle. Next it was Katie and Luke's turn to leave, and she met him in front of the flower-strewn gazebo. He took her hand possessively as they made their way up the aisle and away from the seated guests. Once they reached the reception tent, he stopped and quickly kissed her, his eyes beautifully blue and twinkling. "You look gorgeous."

"So do you, Lucas Boone."

His grin made her dizzy. "I expect to dance with you all night long."

"Don't I get one dance with the groom?"

His mouth twisted adorably. "One, since it's my brother."

Photographers were snapping photos and a videographer was recording the entire event. Katie had a mind to release Luke's hand and hoped the kiss wasn't captured on film. These photos were bound to make the newspapers in Boone County. But as she pulled her hand away slightly, Luke tightened his hold, making it clear he wasn't going to play that game anymore.

It meant she'd have to speak with her mother and sister soon. Like tonight after the wedding, or tomorrow, at the latest.

Chandeliers hung from the high beams and the drapes were parted in strategic places to give the tent an airy feel in the late afternoon. Hors d'oeuvres and champagne were passed around by white-jacketed waiters and Mason and Drea took their places at the head table beside Risk and April. Mason waited until his guests were all inside the reception area before he picked up a microphone.

"May I have your attention please? First of all, I want to thank you all for coming and sharing our special day with us," he said. The crowd settled and all looked his way. "I have an announcement to make. Actually, it's really a wedding present for my bride."

Surprised, Drea gave him a curious look, though her eyes were still glowing.

"Tonight, our musical entertainment will be provided by The Band Blue."

Sean Manfred walked into the tented area, along with the rest on his band.

Drea looked from Sean to Mason, and then tears flowed down her cheeks. "Mason, how did you manage this?"

"He didn't have to twist my arm very hard, Drea," Sean said. "Congratulations to both of you."

Drea gave Sean the biggest hug and turned to Mason. For him, she had a major kiss. It was all so touching and sweet. The Band Blue had played a part in getting Mason and Drea together when they'd all worked on a fundraiser for the Boone County Memorial Hospital. And now here they were after winning their first Grammy, playing at Drea and Mason's wedding.

"Pretty cool," Luke said to Katie.

"It's a wonderful surprise. Did you know?"

He nodded. "I knew. I helped Mason arrange it. It's what best men do, right?"

"Yes, but it's quite a secret to keep."

"No bigger than our secret."

"Yeah, about that, we should talk. After the wedding?"

He played with a strand of her hair, distracting her with the loving way he was looking at her. "I'm all in."

Nine

The Band Blue captured the guests' attention, their country pop music less drawl and more beat. Most of the wedding guests got up and danced like it was the best party they'd ever attended and some stood by in awe just watching the band do their thing. It was almost as if they were attending a concert.

Luke hadn't been joking when he said he'd dance with Katie all night long. She'd never had so much fun, but she wasn't at all sorry when The Band Blue began singing a slow, sexy ballad.

"Twinkle toes, let's dance to this slow one," Luke said.

"Thought you'd never ask," she teased.

She walked into his arms and rested her head on his shoulder. Two hundred and fifty guests had seen them stick together like glue this evening. They'd seen the way Luke looked at her when she was giving her funny little toast and they'd seen the way she hung on his every word when he'd given his toast to the happy couple.

She was sure it would get back to her sister, but there was nothing she could do about it. She couldn't hide her feelings for him anymore and slow dancing with him had lots of pluses. Like breathing in his swoon-worthy masculine scent, being held in his strong, powerful arms and enjoying his occasional and surprising kisses.

The crud would hit the fan later, but right now she wasn't going to think about that. She wanted to celebrate her best friend's wedding without fear or trepidation.

She lifted up on her toes and gave Luke a sweet kiss on the mouth.

He brought her tighter into his embrace. "What was that for?"

She gazed into his eyes. "Just because."

"That's a good enough reason for me."

He always made her smile. Well, not always, but recently she found herself breaking free of the binds of obligation to Shelly and her mom.

"This is probably the best wedding I've ever attended," she said dreamily.

"You mean, ours wasn't this good?"

"Ours? It's not even a blip on my radar."

"I know." He kissed the top of her head. "I'll make that up to you one day."

She gazed at him, finally finding the courage she needed. "Luke, will you come with me?"

"Sure, where are we going?"

"To the gazebo. It should be quiet there. And well, the reception's almost over. We'll be back in time for the last dance."

Luke took her hand and led her down the pathway leading to the gazebo. The sun was just descending, the sky to the west ablaze with hues of pinks and oranges. Once they reached the gazebo, she walked up the steps and took a seat. Luke sat directly beside her.

She got right down to business. "I don't know where to start, but yesterday when I found out you were inside Drew's house with fire all around you, I couldn't deny my feelings for you any longer. I love you, Luke. I don't know when it happened or why. Lord knows, I have half a dozen reasons not to care for you but I do. Very much."

His eyes closed, as if he were treasuring her words, as if he was trying to lock this memory away. He'd been patient with her. And obstinate and persistent. But she loved him, all of him, and she was glad to finally tell him.

"Katie, I've waited five long years for this. I love you. I've already told you but it wasn't the way I wanted to tell you. Not in the heat of an argument like that."

"I kicked you out of my house when you told me."

"I know. And I'll admit now, I overstepped my bounds by denying you competition at the bakery. It's just the way I love. I protect the people I care about."

"But you won't do anything like that again, will you?"

"I promise you, I won't."

She smiled and Luke ran his hands up and down her

arms, soothingly, sweetly, and then he kissed her and kept on kissing her until she could barely breathe. She put a hand on his chest. "There's more."

"Tell me more." His eyes glistened as he gave her his full attention.

"I'm, uh… I'm…pregnant. You're going to be a father."

There, she'd said it. Telling him only made it seem more real.

"Ah, Katie." Tears misted in his eyes. "This is the best news," he said, relieving her qualms. She'd had no idea if he even wanted children. It had never been a topic of conversation. Why would it be, when all she'd been focusing on lately was divorcing him?

"So then, you're okay with it?"

"I'm…blown away. Did you worry I wouldn't be happy about this?"

"I didn't know how you felt about children in general. I've never seen you around them, but I see how compassionate you are around horses and all animals really, so I was hoping this wouldn't rattle you."

"I'm on top of the world right now. You and I created a baby, sweetheart, and I'll love that child as much as I love you. I don't care when or how it happened, it's a blessing."

"I think so, too," she said softly. "But I've always used protection. I'm fuzzy about our wedding night in Vegas."

"Me, too. I, um, I would never put you at risk, Katie. Not consciously. I hope you know that."

"I do. I guess we both blurred out."

"Yeah"

"It's just…well, I'm going to have to face my sister and mom very soon."

"The sooner the better, Katie. And I'll be with you every step of the way."

"T-thanks. But this is something I have to do on my own. Tomorrow. I'm gonna tell them tomorrow. Right now, I think we should get back to the wedding."

"I could sit here all night with you, but you're right." He cupped her face, laid a solid, delicious kiss on her lips and then stared into her eyes. "We should get back."

Hand in hand, they made their way down the gazebo steps approaching the twinkling lights of the tent, just as April came out to greet them holding a cell phone. "Katie, I think this might be important. Your phone's been ringing on the table almost nonstop."

"Oh, okay. Thanks, April." She glanced at her recent calls. "It's from Shelly. I'll be just a minute. Please excuse me." Alarmed, Katie hid her concern from Luke and April. Shelly knew where she was tonight and she wouldn't call unless it was super important.

"Want me to stay?" Luke asked.

"No, you go on. I'm sure it's nothing."

April hooked Luke's arm. "Come on, Luke. You owe me a dance."

Reluctantly Luke was led away and Katie paced back and forth until her sister picked up.

"Shelly? It's me. What's wrong?"

The news was not good. Katie's mom was in the hospital. This time it wasn't her heart, but a case of pneumonia and it was bad enough for Shelly to take her to the emergency room.

Katie took a minute to absorb it all, her heart beating fast, and then she went back to the reception to seek out Luke. She found him just finishing a dance with April. Grabbing his arm, she took him off to the side. "I have to leave. My mom's very ill. She's in the hospital. Will you please tell Drea and Mason I'm sorry, but I have to go?"

"I'll go with you," he said immediately.

"No."

"No? Katie, I'll drive you."

"Goodness, Luke. Don't you get it? I can't show up at the hospital with you."

"Are we back to that?"

"I'm sorry. But I'm going. By myself."

Luke's mouth hardened to a thin line and that stubborn tick twitched in his jaw.

She couldn't deal with him right now. She had to get to the hospital.

Katie sat by her mother's hospital bed, watching her sleep. Her breathing seemed labored right now and she hated seeing her hooked up to all that equipment. Outside in the hallway, she heard Shelly's voice and turned just in time to see her sister speaking to Davis Moore. When they were through talking, Dr. Moore took hold of Shelly's hand and promised to check in with her later.

Shelly gave the good doctor a hero-worship smile, one only a sister would recognize, and kept her eyes trained on him as he walked away.

If her mother wasn't so ill, Katie might find that amusing.

Shelly walked into the room and laid a hand on Katie's shoulder. "You must've come straight from the wedding."

"Your call scared me so I didn't bother to go home to change."

"I'm glad you're here."

She put her hand over the one Shelly had placed on her shoulder. "Of course I'd come."

"You look pretty," Shelly said. "That color suits you."

What? No snide remark about the Boones or the wedding?

"Thank you." Katie rose from her chair to face Shelly. "How's Mom doing?"

"Things have calmed down now. She had a fever when I brought her in and her coughing was bad."

"Thank goodness you were with her tonight."

"I, uh, wasn't. I was out, but I called to check on her and heard her hacking away. I knew it wasn't good. Davis thought that I should take her straight to the emergency room."

Davis? Shelly must've been out with him tonight. And hopefully not at a seminar. "I didn't realize Mom was ill."

"It came on suddenly. She was having trouble breathing and with her fever spiking, I didn't want to take any chances. She's where she needs to be at the moment."

Katie nodded, tears welling in her eyes. Her mother looked pale and so still. Fear stuck in her throat. She couldn't lose her mother. She was too young. She was going to be a grandmother.

Katie's stomach churned, her emotions roiling. Though her eyes burned, she wouldn't cry. She needed to be strong. "Do...do you think she's going to be okay?"

"Pneumonia is never good in an older person, but Mom should be able to recover from this now that she's being monitored," Shelly said in her nurse voice. "I do want to warn you, Mom's health isn't the best in general, so it may take a long time for her to get better."

Katie sighed, pain reaching deep into her heart. "Just as long as she does."

"It's important that she stay calm. She'll be medicated throughout the night. You don't have to stay, Katie. I'll call you if anything changes."

"No, I'm not going home. When Mom wakes up, I want to be here."

"Okay, sis. But at least go home and change your clothes. It gets chilly at night on the hospital floors. You'll freeze in that dress."

Katie hesitated a moment. "I don't want to leave Mom."

"I'll stay until you get back. Mom won't be alone."

"Okay, if you promise."

"Go, little sis. And of course I promise. You can always count on me."

Katie took those words to heart. Her older sister had always been her friend, had always had her back. She'd been someone she could rely on for all their years.

Katie's heart sank even further with guilt. She was torn up inside, worried sick over her mother and worried about Shelly's reaction to her news. All her life, she'd never wanted to let anyone down. And now, it seemed, she was letting down everyone she cared about. "I'll be back in fifteen minutes, at the latest."

She gave her mother an air-kiss and then walked out of the hospital room feeling a sense of desperation and sadness. She hated seeing her mother looking frail and weak.

As she walked toward the elevator, she pulled out her cell phone, ready to let Drea and Luke know what was going on. The screen went black. "Shoot." She was out of charge. Of course. She'd used her phone all day long during the wedding, taking pictures and texting Lori about bakery issues, never realizing she'd need it tonight.

Making her way through the lobby, she found her car easily in the parking lot and drove to her apartment. The drive only took five minutes. As she pulled into her parking space at the back end of the bakery, a car followed her and parked directly next to her. It was Luke.

She got out of her car, and so did he. She met him in front of her back door.

"Katie, I texted and called you and then I started to worry," he said. "What's going on?"

"Luke, I'm in a hurry right now."

"And you couldn't call me?"

"My cell has no charge. It died just as I was texting you and Drea. My mother's really ill right now. I only came home to change my clothes so I can sit with her during the night."

"I'm sorry to hear that. What's wrong with her?"

"Pneumonia. I'm so worried. They've got her hooked up to all these machines. It's scary to look at."

"Ah, that's too bad. Let me help. What can I do?"

He reached for her, and she scooted away. "Nothing. There's really nothing you can do. My mom's recovery could take weeks. Maybe longer. Shelly is waiting for me at the hospital right now."

He ran a hand through his hair. "Katie, why do I get the feeling you're pushing me away again?"

"I'm...not. I just can't focus on more than one problem at a time."

"I'm your problem?"

"You know what I mean. I'm really sorry, but I have to get upstairs."

"Okay, go. But you know how to reach me if you ever need anything."

"I do. Thanks."

She sidestepped him and went to the back door.

"Charge your phone, Katie," he said as he climbed back into his car.

"I will. I'll text you tomorrow."

Luke didn't look happy. He was right—she'd pushed him away. She couldn't afford having him around. How would she explain it? It was the same old same old, except now her mother was in even worse shape than before.

She raced up her stairs and shed her pretty maid of honor gown, throwing on a pair of comfy black leggings and a big cozy gray sweatshirt. She wrapped her feet up in a pair of warm socks and put on tennis shoes.

She had always thought falling in love would be easy

and fun and thrilling. Well, loving Luke had caused her nothing but indecision and pain. It wasn't supposed to be this way. She did love him. The thought of not having him in her life destroyed her.

And she feared if she pushed Luke too far, he'd never come back.

When Luke returned to the ranch, he found his family sitting at a table under the tent, drinking a final toast to Mason and Drea. All the guests were gone. The caterers and waiters were just leaving and the tent was due to be taken down tomorrow.

The lights still twinkled, clashing with his dark mood.

He brought over a bottle of Jack Daniels from the bar and sat next to Risk.

All eyes were on him, including his Aunt Lottie's and Drew's.

"How is Katie's mother?" Drea asked.

"She's in the hospital with pneumonia."

"Oh no. Poor Diana. First a heart attack and now this. Is she bad?"

"According to Katie, she is. She's worried sick." Luke slouched in the chair and sipped from the bottle, raising a few eyebrows. He didn't care. He needed his family to know the truth. It was time. "My wife doesn't want me there."

His brothers exchanged glances and then Mason asked, "I'm sorry, did you say wife?"

"Yep. I married Katie in Las Vegas." He sipped from the bottle again.

"What," Mason asked, "are you talking about?"

"I'm married to Katie. It's true."

"I'm in shock," Risk said, glancing at April.

"No more than she was when she woke up next to me in Vegas."

"Wow, bro. You got married during my bachelor party?" Mason said.

"Yeah, I did."

"Okay. Well, Katie is a great person." Mason put out his hand and they shook on it. "Congratulations."

"Same here," Risk said, slapping him on the back. "Congrats."

Luke frowned. "Don't get carried away. It's not a marriage made in heaven. It was one of those too-drunk-to-know-any-better moments. Immediately, Katie demanded a divorce." He gulped down another swig of whiskey, finally feeling the effects of the alcohol.

"Well, I think you and Katie are meant for each other. You two make a great couple," April said sweetly.

It only made him feel worse. "She thinks her mother and Shelly would never accept it. She swore me to secrecy. She didn't want the word to get out. The truth is, I love her and she loves me. But it's taken a lot of persuasion on my part to get her to admit it." He gave everyone at the table an equal glance. "I'm sorry I haven't told you before this."

"So why now?" Aunt Lottie asked.

"Why now?" He gave them all another look. "Because Katie is pregnant. We're having a baby."

"Wow! This is amazing. The best wedding present you could have given us," Mason said, pulling Luke up and hugging him. "And I didn't think anything could top you getting The Band Blue here."

Drea stood, too, and they embraced. "I'm so happy for you and Katie."

"I can't believe it. This is wonderful news," April said.

Risk pulled him in for a hug. "Wow, you sure know how to liven up a party. Congrats." He slapped him on the back. "Hey, I'm gonna be an uncle."

Tears swam in Drea's and April's eyes. "We're gonna be aunts," they said at the same time as if just realizing it, and then everyone laughed.

When the laughter died down, Luke shook his head, grateful for their encouragement. "And now for the hard part. I'm gonna have to swear you all to secrecy. Just until Katie feels like she can share the news with Diana and Shelly. Right now, she won't hear of it. And she's doing her best to push me away, too."

"Why?" April asked. "If she loves you?"

"It's what women do sometimes," Lottie said sagely, glancing at Drew.

April nodded. "Yeah, I guess I did that with Risk, too."

"And I did that to Mason," Drea said. "But we all had good reasons, at the time. Just don't give up on her. She does love you."

"How can you be so sure of that?" Mason asked his new wife.

Drea kissed his cheek and said softly, "Best friends know these things." Then she turned to Luke. "I'm sure of it."

"Thanks, and don't worry. I've been very patient with Katie. She was ready to tell her family the truth until Diana got sick. I won't let her push me too far away. I have a plan."

"A Boone with a plan? Just make sure it doesn't backfire," Aunt Lottie said.

He'd had the same thought. But he had to try something.

His patience was at an end.

Katie was on a roll this morning. She'd finished baking cupcakes and frosted one hundred of them in less than an hour in her work kitchen. They were now ready to go in the dessert case.

"Lori, cupcakes are up."

"Coming," Lori called from the bakery. "I'll be right there."

Katie washed the bowls and utensils, and when Lori walked in she grabbed one of the large cupcake tins. "Wow. Working fast."

"I have to. I'm going to stop by the hospital to check on my mom after the morning rush. Thank you for holding down the fort for me this week."

"Of course. How's Mama doing today?"

"Getting better every day. Her doctor says she's out of danger."

"All good news."

"I know. Thank goodness. Her fever is gone and if it stays normal for one more day, they'll release her."

Katie had closed the bakery for the first three days while her mother was fighting pneumonia and had taken turns with Shelly to sit with her at the hospital. She re-opened her shop once her mom's recovery took a good turn.

"That's great, Katie. It's been a hard week for you."

"As long as my mom gets to come home, it's all worth it."

"I'll keep good thoughts for her."

"Thanks."

Once Lori walked out, Katie checked her cell phone. No texts yet from Luke. He usually texted her first thing in the morning and then at night before bed. He always asked about her mother's health, and made sure she was feeling okay, too. She hadn't seen him since the wedding and it was killing her. She really missed him, but not enough to ask him to come over.

She couldn't take the pressure right now and she understood that this wasn't the way Luke wanted it. He wanted to be let into her heart and her life. She wasn't sure if Luke was trying to abide by her wishes by staying away, or if he was really angry with her. Maybe a little bit of both.

"Oh God," she murmured. She didn't want to push him away like this, but what choice did she have?

The morning rush was intense, Katie and Lori working their butts off, trying to accommodate all the customers' orders. Davis Moore walked in and Katie waved to him.

He gave her a quick smile. "Hi, Katie."

"Hi, Davis. Are you here for your usual?"

He'd become a regular customer and she had gotten to know him a bit. "Actually, I'm surprising the entire floor with your cupcakes this morning. Can you pack up two dozen for me to take back to the staff?"

"Sure." She turned to Lori. "We can do that, right?"

Lori nodded, getting two big boxes ready.

"Be sure to include Shelly's favorite, lemon raspberry," he told her. "Put in two of those. Your sister got me hooked on them, too."

"Shelly's good for business."

He grinned. "She's good all the way around."

Katie paused momentarily, holding back a wide smile. "I agree."

"Your mom's making progress on her recovery. I checked in on her this morning."

"Thank you. It makes me feel good knowing she's getting expert care. Actually, I'll be leaving here in just a few minutes to visit her."

"I wouldn't rush. She's got a visitor right now."

"Oh yeah? Do you know who it is?" Katie asked, making conversation as she totaled up the bill at the cash register.

"Well, someone told me it was Shelly's ex. He walked in with a big bouquet of tulips for your mom."

Katie nearly swallowed her tongue. Luke had gone to see her mother with a bouquet of her favorite flowers? "Davis, you know what? These cupcakes are on the house. As a thank-you to you and the rest of the staff."

"Well, that's nice of you—"

"Lori will finish up your order." Katie removed her apron and grabbed her purse. "I actually can't wait to see Mama another minute. I'll be back later," she told Lori. "Bye, Davis."

Then she dashed out the door, her stomach gripping tight. It wasn't morning sickness making her ill. It was a heavy dose of dread.

What in hell was Luke up to?

Ten

Luke hoped he wasn't making a big mistake. He stood outside Diana Rodgers's hospital room and took a breath. Holding a bouquet of Diana's favorite flowers in one hand, he gave her door a little tap with the other.

After a brief pause, she said, "Come in."

Her voice sounded strong. According to Katie, Diana was doing well. She'd make a full recovery and might even go home tomorrow. *Here goes,* he thought. He'd gotten the okay from Diana's nurse to pay her a visit.

He walked through the slightly open door and found her sitting up in bed. She glanced at him and the softness in her eyes disappeared. "Luke, what are you doing here?"

"May I come in?"

"You already have."

He nodded and set the tulips down on the bedside table. "For you."

Grudgingly, she glanced at the flowers. "They're lovely."

"I remembered your favorite."

She half smiled. "If only you'd remembered to marry my daughter."

Luke stared at her, understanding her wrath. "I came to speak with you, Diana. If you would hear me out."

"Haven't we said all there is to say years ago?"

"No, I don't think so."

Diana looked better than he expected. Her face hinted at a rosy sheen, her hazel eyes were bright and she seemed to have attitude, which he remembered about her. She was never a pushover.

"If you want me to leave, I will. But first, I want to say I'm glad to see you're making a full recovery. You look good."

"Thank you for that." She folded her arms over her chest.

"I'm here to speak to you about Katie."

"Katie? What about Katie?" Diana's eyes shifted warily.

"Well… Katie and I have been friends now a long time."

"I know. She always defends you."

"She does?" That made him smile. "I suppose I'm not your favorite person. But I'm here to explain about what happened. You see, I did love Shelly. I thought she was right for me and I was right for her. I suppose I'll always hold a special place in my heart for her."

"She was sick for months after you broke off the engagement. She crawled into a shell and didn't come out for a long time."

Luke pulled up a chair and took a bedside seat. "I'm sorry about that. But you might say I did the same by joining the Marines. I was hiding out, too, in my own way."

"And what were you hiding from?"

"My feelings. You see, I didn't mean it to happen and I certainly didn't want it to happen, but I fell deeply in love—"

"With another woman?" she asked quietly.

"Yes. I fell hard. I couldn't help it. This girl was everything I was looking for. She was bright and independent and funny. We shared the same interests and—"

"My Katie?"

"Yessss." Luke closed his eyes briefly, then opened them to look straight at Diana. "I'm in love with Katie. It's the real reason I left town. I didn't want to come between Katie and her sister. I left my family, my work, all the things I loved, to keep peace in your family. She never knew. She never encouraged me."

Diana bit her lip and then sighed. "Now that explains it. We couldn't figure out why you broke up with Shelly days before the wedding. And you didn't stick around long enough to work things out with her. You left her high and dry."

"I know. I've apologized to her and to you. Many times. And well, I did a good job of staying away from Katie when I returned home to Boone Springs, except for the time we'd spend at Red Barrel together. Katie was the perfect protective sister. She never gave an inch and I accepted that. But then we were thrown together for Mason's wedding."

"And?"

"And I fell in love with him, Mama."

Katie entered the room and set a hand on Luke's shoulder. She gave him a look that said she'd take it from here *and don't you dare argue*. He wouldn't dream of it.

"You love Luke?"

"I do, Mama. He's a good man."

Her mother continued to nibble on her lip. "What about Shelly?"

"I'll speak with her tonight."

"Brave."

"I'm not, Mama. I should've told you the whole truth myself. You see, Luke and I got married in Las Vegas during the bachelorette party weekend. A little too much tequila at night makes a girl do silly things. I was beside myself and panicked when I woke up seeing that marriage license. I was worried sick about how you and Shelly would take it."

"She tried to divorce me," he said. "But I stalled her."

"You stalled her until she fell in love with you?" Diana asked.

"Yes." He kissed the top of Katie's hand and looked into her beautiful eyes. She'd finally come around and nothing made him happier. "I couldn't let her go a second time. I love her too much."

"Mama, I finally realized my love for Luke when he ran into that burning house and saved Drew's life.

He could've been killed in that fire and all of a sudden, everything became clear to me."

"I see. I read about your heroics in the newspaper, Luke. It was courageous of you. And what you sacrificed to spare Shelly's feelings is commendable. You stayed away from home for four years. You did an honorable thing. It makes me feel a little bit ashamed about how I've treated you."

"Don't be. I understand."

"You can't help who you fall in love with, Mama."

"I guess not."

"There's more," Katie said.

Luke stood up, grateful that Katie was finally revealing the entire truth. He wrapped his arm around her shoulder and brought her in close, showing solidarity.

"We're going to have a baby, Mama," she said. "You're going to be a grandmother."

Diana's eyes went wide for a few seconds, as if sorting out the words in her head, and once the shock wore off, a big smile graced her face. "You're pregnant?"

"Yes, Mama. And you're going to be the best Grammy ever."

"That's wonderful news, sweetheart. I can hardly believe my little girl is going to be a mother. And I'm going to be a grandmother." Diana put out her arms, and Katie ran into them. "All I've ever wanted is for my girls to be happy."

"I am, Mama. I'm very happy."

"Then so am I."

When Katie backed away, Diana stretched out her arms again. "Luke?"

He walked over to her and she hugged him tight. He'd always liked Diana, and she'd treated him like part of the family when he was with Shelly. Was it possible to regain that bond again? "I guess…you're my son-in-law now."

"Guess so."

"Well then, welcome to the family, Lucas Boone," Diana said. "In a million years, I never thought I'd say those words to you."

Luke felt a thousand times better than when he'd first walked in here. "Neither did I."

Katie knocked on Shelly's apartment door. She'd had this place ever since college; it was in a nice neighborhood surrounded by parks and gardens. Shelly had done well for herself. She'd become a highly respected nurse and was on her way to bigger things professionally. While Katie nurtured horses and all animals, Shelly loved patient care. She had a nurturing spirit, too, and it had taken her a long time after her breakup to get back to a good place in her life again.

Katie's nerves rattled as she waited for Shelly to answer the door. She prayed that her news wouldn't set her sister back. That had been her greatest fear of all—that her sister would be crushed all over again.

When Shelly opened the door, she seemed surprised. "Katie? I was just going to the hospital to give you a break. What is it? Is something wrong with Mom?"

"No, nothing's wrong with Mom. She's actually feeling much better."

"Oh good. For a second there, I got worried."

"Can I come in?"

Shelly's brows furrowed and she stepped aside to let Katie in. "That expression on your face has me puzzled. You look...scared. Are you shaking?"

"I, uh. Shelly, we need to talk."

"Okay," she said. "What's up?"

Katie's legs went weak and she took a seat on the living room sofa. She'd rehearsed what she would say to Shelly many times, but as hard as this confession was in her head, it was ten times harder in person. "I have something to tell you, Shel. But first I want you to know I love you very much and I'd never intentionally hurt you."

"Of course, I know that. Same here. Please tell me what's on your mind, because I'm starting to get a weird vibe here."

"Weird? No, that's not the word I'd use."

"Katie, you're being cryptic."

"Okay, okay. It's just hard to begin. It's about... Luke."

Shelly blinked a few times. "What about Luke?"

"I, uh, he's my... Remember, I love you."

She nodded.

"Well, when Luke came back home from overseas last year, we started bumping into each other at the rescue. It wasn't a friendship really, but we shared a mutual love for horses and we worked together there at times. But it never went beyond that. I swear to you. Then in Vegas, during the party for Mason and Drea, Luke and I both got blistering drunk. Luke offered to walk me back to the hotel. Only we didn't quite make it back. Instead…we went to the Midnight Chapel and… got…married."

Shelly's eyes nearly bulged out of her head. "You got married? Am I hearing correctly? You and Luke are married?"

Bile rose in her throat. The last thing she wanted was to cause her sister grief. She took a breath and went on, "I t-tried to get a divorce, but Luke kept stalling me, saying his attorney wasn't available. And I didn't know what to do. Shel, I was panicked. We hid it from everyone. I just wanted the ordeal to be over. Luke and I were thrown together a lot because of Drea's wedding. And when Snow died, we bonded over that. And well, Luke shared with me the real reason he couldn't marry you. It killed me to hear it. But you have to know the whole truth. Luke had fallen in love…with me," she whispered.

Shelly seemed unusually calm, but Katie didn't take that as a good sign. "Luke fell in love with you?"

"Again, Shel, I never encouraged him back then. We were friends. He was going to be my brother-in-law. And well, that's when he decided to break up with you and join the Marines. He didn't want to hurt you anymore than he had. He left his home and family so that he wouldn't come between us. He kept away for four years and when he returned home… Well, you know the rest. I'm so sorry, Shelly. I didn't want this to come between us. Ever."

"Well, what did you think would happen? That I'd be jumping for joy?"

"No, just the opposite. That's why this is so hard."

"I was a mess after he dumped me. And you're telling me you knew nothing about this?"

"I truly didn't. I swear. I was just as shocked when he told me the truth as you are now. And I didn't want any part of it. I fought my feelings for him."

Shelly ground her teeth, trying for restraint but Katie knew that look. Her sister wanted to scream to high heaven at the injustice of it all. How could she blame her? She'd held on to her bitterness for all these years. *"Your feelings for him?"*

Katie sighed deeply. "Yes, I have feelings for Luke. I love him. I mean, I didn't know that I'd fallen in love with him, until he ran into a burning building to save Drew MacDonald's life. After that, I realized how much he meant to me. How much I cared for him. How much it would hurt if I lost him."

"And so, you threw your sister under the bus for a guy."

Her words cut deep, but Shelly's anger seemed to lessen, and was there actually space between her tight lips now? Was she making a joke?

Katie reached for her sister's hands and hung on tight.

"Your hands are freezing," Shelly said. "You're really tortured about this, aren't you?"

"Of course I am." Katie held back a sob.

"I hate seeing you in such pain."

"And I hate knowing I've caused you pain. I know you have no use for Luke."

"You shouldn't have to choose between us."

"But you only have horrible things to say about him,

Shel. And I know this is awkward as hell, but... I don't know what to do."

Shelly sat quietly for a while, holding her ice cold hands, thinking. Seconds seemed like hours, but then her sister released a big breath.

"You *know* what to do," Shelly said firmly. "You love him and he loves you. There's nothing to do except make a life with him. Look, I know I've been bitter, and I've been difficult. I was hurt, but I finally realized that I didn't want a man who didn't love me like crazy. What kind of marriage would that make? Luke wasn't right for me. Not the way..."

"Davis is?" Katie asked, hopefully.

Shelly sighed. "We're getting closer every day. He's amazing."

"The feeling is mutual, on his part. Whenever he comes into the bakery, he finds a way to tell me just that."

Shelly had a dreamy look on her face. "He does?"

"Yep. Every single time."

"We have the same interests and, well, we're taking it slow, but I've never felt this way about anyone before. Davis always makes me feel special."

"That's wonderful, Shelly. I'm really happy for you." Katie nibbled on her lips, hesitating. "But I have another bit of news. I'm afraid there's more."

Shelly tilted her head. "Can I handle more news?"

"Gosh, I hope so. This is important." She laid a hand on her abdomen, a protective gesture that any woman would pick up on, especially a nurse.

The words wouldn't come. This news could crush her sister and ruin their relationship for good.

But it seemed she didn't have to speak the words. Shelly's eyes riveted to her stomach and *she knew.* "You're pregnant."

Goodness, this was difficult. "H-how do you feel about becoming an aunt?"

"An aunt. Katie?"

"Yes, I'm, uh, we're going to have a baby, Shel. I hope this isn't too much for you, because I'm really gonna need you. I need my big sis."

"My gosh, Katie. This is a lot to take in."

"I know," she squeaked, and gave Shelly her best little sister pout. It used to work when they were kids. "But I hope you can, 'cause I'm gonna really need you."

Shelly's shoulders relaxed and her expression changed. "You know what? I'm through being miserable. It's like meeting Davis has shined a bright light inside me. So, yes, of course I'll be there for you. You're my baby sister."

Tears dripped freely down Katie's face as she gave her sister a gigantic heartfelt squeeze. "Oh Shel, this means everything to me. Thank you."

"Have you told Mom?"

"Yes, just before I spoke with you," Katie said. "She's gonna be a grandma, and that makes her happy. I think she's accepted Luke, too. She said she just wants her girls to be happy."

Shelly smiled for the first time since Katie walked into the apartment. "Then, I think she's gotten her wish."

When Katie arrived home, she slumped on her bed, drained of energy. It had been an emotional day and all she could think about was getting into bed and falling asleep. It didn't matter it was only six in the evening, she was bone weary.

Her cell phone buzzed and buzzed and she dug into her purse. It was Luke. Immediately, she smiled. Her husband was calling.

She chuckled and then answered the phone. "Hi," she said.

"Hi."

Just hearing his voice brought her peace.

"How did it go with your sister?"

"It was difficult, but Shelly will come around. She's in love with someone and I think it's going to be okay."

Luke released a big sigh. "Glad to hear it, sweetheart. That makes this day perfect. Well, almost perfect. If you look outside now, you'll see there's a car waiting for you out front."

"A car? Luke, what are you up to?"

"You'll see. The driver knows where to take you. Trust me, Katie."

She took a deep breath. "Can I have twenty minutes? I need to shower and change."

"Okay, but remember I'll be waiting."

After she hung up the phone, she took a quick shower and put on her favorite floral sundress, one that wouldn't be fitting her too much longer. She tossed a short denim jacket over the dress and then slipped her feet into a pair of tan leather boots. Then she brushed her hair to one side and let it flow down her shoulders. She stared into the mirror for a second, wondering how on earth she'd gotten to this point in her life. This time, her thoughts weren't filled with dread and fear but with hope and promise.

The "car" Luke had sent was a limousine. Of course. At times she forgot how incredibly wealthy he was. The driver opened the door for her and she climbed in the back seat and stretched out.

"Miss, there's food and snacks and apple cider in case you get hungry," the driver said.

"Why, where am I going? Is it far?"

"Not too far. Mr. Boone wanted to make sure you were comfortable."

"I am, thank you. So, you can't tell me where you're taking me?"

"And ruin the surprise?" he asked with a grin before closing her door.

Surprise? Goodness, she didn't know how much more her heart could take today, but she leaned back, closed her eyes and relaxed. Luke had asked her to trust him. And she did.

A short time later, the limo turned down the path toward Red Barrel Horse Rescue. Katie sat up straighter in the seat and peered out the window. Her curiosity aroused, she scanned the area. There was no sign of Luke. The driver parked in front of the office and then got out to open the door for her. "Miss, Mr. Boone is waiting for you in the barn."

She glanced over to the big red barn and saw Luke approaching, wearing his black Stetson and a stunning dark suit, a string tie at his neck. Her heart raced. He was handsome and wonderful and all hers. She picked up the pace and soon she was in his arms, his mouth devouring hers, laying claim, making every bone in her body melt.

"Luke," she murmured between kisses. "What's this all about?"

Luke kissed her one last time. "Come with me."

He placed his hand on her back and led her into the barn. She gasped when she saw what he'd done. A dozen arrangements of flowers and tiny white lights surrounded a round linen-clad table set for two. Sparkling cider sat in a bucket of ice. The whole place appeared magical. "This is beautiful."

"I hoped you'd like it."

"But what are we—"

Luke dropped to one knee and took her hands in his. "Katie, I want to do this right. I want you to have all the things a bride should have, including a proper proposal."

"Oh, Luke." Tears swam in her eyes.

"I brought you here because this is where I fell in love with you. We have good memories here, you and me. It's fitting that this is the place I bare my soul to you. Katie Rodgers Boone, I'm crazy in love with you and have been for a long time. You're the only girl for me and I'm asking if you'll have me for your husband. To live and love with me for the rest of our lives. Will you, Katie?"

He reached into his pocket and presented her with a ring. Not just any diamond ring—this one was designed with emerald and marquise cuts of diamonds in the shape of a barrel. Red rubies surrounded the whole ring. "Do you see it?" he asked.

Tears streamed down her face now. Her every dream was coming true. "I see it. It's very special. And I see you for the good and honorable man that you are. I love the ring and yes, yes, yes. I'll have you for my husband, if you'll have me as your wife."

A smile spread across his face and he rose up. "Are you joking?" he teased as he placed the ring on her finger. Then he kissed her, a good, long, joyful kiss that warmed her heart. "You're all I've ever wanted. You, me and our baby, Katie, we'll be a family. I can't wait. But for now, I'm grateful our families know about us. We can stop pretending."

"Yes, I'm glad about that, too. I love you very much and now I get to show it."

"There's more."

"There always seems to be with you."

He chuckled and took her hand again. As they walked out of the barn, the sky was a shock of tangerine and pink hues, as if Mother Nature had summoned up such wonder for this moment.

"Katie, I said I didn't want you to miss out on being a bride. So today I'm giving you your wedding present."

"It's not necessary. You've already given me too much."

"Not even close, sweetheart. And I think you're going to like this gift." He led her to Cinnamon's corral. The horse looked her way, those big brown eyes capturing her attention. "I made arrangements to adopt her. She'll be yours."

"Really?" She'd never dared to dream of having a horse of her own. She loved every horse at the rescue, even the feisty ones, but she had a feeling Cinnamon was extra special. "She'll be mine…"

"Yes. And when she's ready, we'll take her to Rising Springs. I've already contacted a trainer to work with her."

"Luke, I don't know what to say but thank you." She buried her face in his shoulder and hugged him tight. "This is all so very much."

He put his hand over her belly. Any day now, the evidence of their love would be pushing the limits of her body and bumping out. "I love this little one already," he said.

She placed her hand over his. "Me, too."

He spoke softly, his arm snugly around her. "We should go in and have our dinner. Gotta keep the baby nourished."

"We do," she said. "And afterward?"

He kissed her, leading her inside. "Afterward, we'll have a proper start to our honeymoon, making hay inside the barn."

Katie laughed as Luke closed the big barn doors.

She was one lucky girl. Waking up wed to the Texan sure had its perks.

Epilogue

Three months later

Drew and Lottie stood before the minister in front of the backyard gazebo on Rising Springs Ranch, saying heartfelt vows of love and devotion. Luke looked on with Katie beside him. Her peach chiffon bridesmaid dress rounded over her growing belly, and her expression was light, bright and happy. The sight of her carrying their child always put a smile on his face and reminded him of his great fortune having married her.

Drea stood as Lottie's maid of honor and Mason as Drew's best man. Risk and April were also in the wedding party, along with a few of Drew and Lottie's good friends.

"I do," said Lottie, staring blissfully into Drew Mac-

Donald's eyes. Drew was eager to repeat those same vows to her. The wedding was a family affair with fewer than thirty people in attendance. It was how Drew and Lottie wanted it. Only the most special people in their lives had received an invitation.

Theirs was the final piece of the puzzle that was the Boone family.

Drew's cottage was under repair, with the addition of new rooms and a modern kitchen for Lottie. The renovations gave the whole place a face-lift and soon, their Tuesday night poker games would resume there.

Mason and Drea had just moved into their newly built home on the property. Word had it that Drea was eager to start a family and Mason was more than willing to oblige.

Risk and April were just finishing the work at Canyon Lake Lodge, hoping to open their new venture this June. The Boones would receive the first invitation to test out the lodge, before paying customers made reservations.

Luke and Katie were living at the ranch, his wife delegating duties between Lori and a new hire at her shop. She didn't want to give up Katie's Kupcakes entirely, and on her workdays they stayed at Katie's apartment. Things would get a little more complicated when their baby came, but they'd work it out. He had no doubt.

"You may kiss the bride," Minister Gavin declared.

Drew landed a passionate kiss on Lottie's lips, one that made the minister turn a shade of bright red. He pronounced them husband and wife and the couple turned to their guests.

"Ladies and gentlemen, I give you Mr. and Mrs. MacDonald."

Luke took Katie's hand and squeezed it tight as applause broke out for the newly married couple. Katie gazed at him, her pretty green eyes clear and full of love.

As the wedding party and guests dispersed, heading toward the reception area, Luke tugged Katie away to a private corner of the yard. "What is it?" she asked.

"Just wanted a kiss, the good kind."

She laughed and then obliged him, her mouth sweet on his. The touch of her lips never failed to make him fall even harder in love with her. "I love you," he said from deep in his heart.

"I love you right back, Luke," she said sweetly. "And you still make me nutty."

"I still do?"

"Yes, you still do, and I wouldn't have it any other way."

* * * * *

Don't miss a single
Boone Brothers of Texas story
by USA TODAY *bestselling author*
Charlene Sands!

Texan for the Taking
Stranded and Seduced
Vegas Vows, Texas Nights

Available from Harlequin Desire!

WE HOPE YOU ENJOYED THIS BOOK!

HARLEQUIN® Desire

Experience sensual stories of juicy drama and intense chemistry cast in the world of the American elite.

Discover six new books every month, available wherever books are sold!

Harlequin.com

SPECIAL EXCERPT FROM

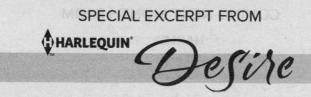

Nadia Jordan certainly didn't plan on spending the
night with Grayson Chandler during the blackout, but
the bigger surprise comes when he introduces her as his
fake fiancée to avoid his family's matchmaking! But even
a fake relationship can't hide their real chemistry...

Read on for a sneak peek at
Blame It on the Billionaire
by USA TODAY bestselling author Naima Simone!

"Do we know each other?"

Her sharp but low intake of breath glanced off his ears, and he
faced her again, openly scrutinizing her face for any telltale signs of
deception. But she was good. Aside from that gasp, her expression
remained shuttered. Either she had nothing to hide or she was damn
good at lying.

He couldn't decide which one to believe.

"No," she whispered. "We don't know each other."

Truth rang in her voice, and the vise squeezing his chest loosened
a fraction of an inch.

"And I guess I didn't see the point of exchanging names. If not
for this blackout or you being in this hallway instead of the ballroom,
our paths wouldn't have crossed. And when the power is restored,
we'll become strangers again. Getting to know each other will pass
the time, but it's not because we truly want to. It's not…honest."

Her explanation struck him like a punch. It echoed throughout his
body, vibrating through skin and bone. Honest. What did he know
about that?

In the world he moved in, deception was everywhere—from the
social niceties of "It's so good to see you" to the cagey plans to land
a business deal. He wasn't used to her brand of frankness, and so he
didn't give her platitudes. Her honesty deserved more than that.

"You're right," he said. "And you're wrong." Deliberately, he straightened his legs until they sprawled out in front him, using that moment to force himself to give her the truth. "If not for me needing to get out of that ballroom and bumping into you here, we wouldn't have met. You would be outside, unprotected in the parking lot or on the road. And I would be trapped in the dark with people I wish I didn't know, most likely going out of my mind. So for that alone, I'm glad we did connect. Because, Nadia…" He surrendered to the need that had been riding him since looking down into her upturned face and clasped a lock of her hair, twisting it around his finger. "Nadia, I would rather be out here with you, a complete stranger I've met by serendipity, than surrounded by the familiar strangers I've known for years in that ballroom."

She stared at him, her pretty lips slightly parted, eyes widened in surprise.

"Another thing you're correct and incorrect about. True, when the lights come back on and we leave here, we probably won't see each other again. But in this moment, there's nothing I want more than to discover more about Nadia with the gorgeous mouth and the unholy curves."

Maybe he shouldn't have pushed it with the comments about her mouth and body, but if they were being truthful, then he refused to hide how attractive he found her. Attractive, hell. Such an anemic description for his hunger to explore every inch of her and be able to write a road map later.

Her lashes fluttered before lowering, hiding her eyes. In her lap, her elegant fingers twisted. He released the strands of her hair and checked the impulse to tip her chin up and order her to look at him.

"Why did you need to escape the ballroom?" she asked softly.

He didn't immediately reply, instead waiting until her gaze rose to meet his.

Only then did he whisper, "To find you."

Find out what happens next in
Blame It on the Billionaire
by USA TODAY *bestselling author Naima Simone.*

Available February 2020 wherever
Harlequin® Desire books and ebooks are sold.

Harlequin.com

Love Harlequin romance?

DISCOVER.

Be the first to find out about promotions, news and exclusive content!

Facebook.com/HarlequinBooks

Twitter.com/HarlequinBooks

Instagram.com/HarlequinBooks

Pinterest.com/HarlequinBooks

ReaderService.com

EXPLORE.

Sign up for the Harlequin e-newsletter and download a free book from any series at **TryHarlequin.com.**

CONNECT.

Join our Harlequin community to share your thoughts and connect with other romance readers!
Facebook.com/groups/HarlequinConnection

**ROMANCE WHEN
YOU NEED IT**

HSOCIAL2018